Without realization, Tia was winding her hand around Anatole's waist.

He laid her back across his lap, half supported on his arm as he kissed her still, one hand palming her swelling breast until she moaned, eyes closed, her face filled with an expression of bliss he would have had to be blind not to see. He lifted his mouth from hers, let his eyes feast on her a moment, before his mouth descended yet again to graze on the line of her cheekbones, to nip at the tender lobes of her ears.

He let his hand slip reluctantly from her breast and then slide languorously along her flank to rest on her thigh, to smooth away the light cotton of her skirt until his hand found the bare skin beneath. To stroke and to caress and to hear her moan again, to feel her thigh strain against him—feel, too, his own body surge to full arousal.

Desire flamed in him...strong, impossible to resist...

Secret Heirs of Billionaires

There are some things money can't buy...

Living life at lightning pace, these magnates are no strangers to stakes at their highest. It seems they've got it all... That is, until they find out that there's an unplanned item to add to their list of accomplishments!

Achieved:

1. Successful business empire.

2. Beautiful women in their bed.

3. *An heir to bear their name?*

Though every billionaire needs to leave his legacy in safe hands, discovering a secret heir shakes up the carefully orchestrated plan in more ways than one!

Uncover their secrets in:

The Desert King's Secret Heir by Annie West

The Sheikh's Secret Son by Maggie Cox

The Innocent's Shameful Secret by Sara Craven

The Greek's Pleasurable Revenge by Andie Brock

The Secret Kept from the Greek by Susan Stephens

Carrying the Spaniard's Child by Jennie Lucas

Kidnapped for the Tycoon's Baby by Louise Fuller

Look out for more stories in the
Secret Heirs of Billionaires series coming soon!

Julia James

THE GREEK'S SECRET SON

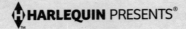

Recycling programs for this product may not exist in your area.

ISBN-13: 978-1-335-41918-7

The Greek's Secret Son

First North American Publication 2018

Copyright © 2018 by Julia James

For questions and comments about the quality of this book, please contact us at CustomerService@Harlequin.com.

Printed in U.S.A.

Julia James lives in England and adores the peaceful verdant countryside and the wild shores of Cornwall. She also loves the Mediterranean—so rich in myth and history, with its sunbaked landscapes and olive groves, ancient ruins and azure seas. "The perfect setting for romance!" she says. "Rivaled only by the lush tropical heat of the Caribbean—palms swaying by a silver-sand beach lapped by turquoise waters...what more could lovers want?"

Books by Julia James

Harlequin Presents

A Cinderella for the Greek
A Tycoon to Be Reckoned With
Captivated by the Greek
The Forbidden Touch of Sanguardo
Securing the Greek's Legacy
Painted the Other Woman
The Dark Side of Desire
From Dirt to Diamonds
Forbidden or For Bedding?
His Penniless Beauty
The Greek's Million-Dollar Baby Bargain
Greek Tycoon, Waitress Wife

Mistress to Wife

Claiming His Scandalous Love-Child
Carrying His Scandalous Heir

Visit the Author Profile page
at Harlequin.com for more titles.

To all care-workers everywhere. And how grateful we are to them. Thank you to you all.

CHAPTER ONE

A FINE DRIZZLE was threatening. Low cloud loured over the country churchyard and the wintry air was damp and chill as Christine stood beside the freshly dug grave. Grief tore at her for the kindly man who had come to her rescue when the one man on earth she'd most craved had been lost to her. But now Vasilis Kyrgiakis was gone, his heart having finally failed as it had long threatened to do. Turning her from wife to widow.

The word tolled in her mind as she stood, head bowed, a lonely figure. Everyone had been very kind to her for Vasilis had been well regarded, even though she was aware that it had been cause for comment that she had been so much younger than her middle-aged husband. But since the most prominent family in the neighbourhood, the Barcourts, had accepted their Greek-born neighbour and his young wife, so had everyone else.

For her part, Christine had been fiercely loyal—grateful—to her husband, even at this final office for him, and felt her eyes misting with tears as the vicar spoke the words of the committal and the coffin was lowered slowly into the grave.

'We therefore commit his body to the ground, earth to earth, ashes to ashes, dust to dust, in sure and certain hope of the Resurrection...'

The vicar gave his final blessing and then he was guiding her away, with the soft thud of earth falling on wood behind her.

Eyes blurred, she felt herself stumble suddenly, lifting her head to steady herself. Her gaze darted outwards, to the lychgate across the churchyard, where so lately her husband's body had rested before its slow procession from the hearse beyond into the church.

And she froze, with a sense of arctic chill.

A car had drawn up beside the hearse—black, too, with dark-tinted windows. And standing beside it, his suit as black as the hearse, his figure tall, unmoving, was a man she knew well. A man she had not seen for five long years.

The last man in the world she wanted to see again.

Anatole stood motionless, watching the scene play out in the churchyard. Emotions churned within him, but his gaze was fixed only on the slight, slender figure, all in black, standing beside the priest in his long white robe at the open grave of his uncle. The uncle he had not seen—had refused to see—since the unbelievable folly of his marriage.

Anger stabbed at him.

At himself.

At the woman who had trapped his vulnerable uncle into marrying her.

He still did not know how, and it had been *his* fault that she had done so.

I did not see what ambition I was engendering.

It was an ambition that had spawned her own attempt to trap him—when thwarted, she had catastrophically turned on his hapless uncle. The uncle who—a life-long bachelor, a mild-mannered scholar, with none of the wary suspicions that Anatole himself had cultivated throughout his life—had proved an easy target for her.

His gaze rested on her now, as she became aware of his presence. Her expression showed naked shock. Then, with an abrupt movement, he wheeled about, threw himself inside his car and, with a spray of gravel, pulled away, accelerating down the quiet country lane.

Emotion churned again, plunging him back into the past.

Five long years ago...

Anatole drummed his fingers frustratedly on the dashboard. The London rush-hour traffic was gridlocked and had come to a halt, even in this side street. But it was not just the traffic jam that was putting him in a bad mood. It was the prospect of the evening ahead.

With Romola.

His obsidian-dark eyes glinted with unsuppressed annoyance and his sculpted mouth tightened. She was eyeing him up as marriage material. *That* was precisely what he did not welcome.

Marriage was the last thing he wanted! Not for him—no, thank you!

His eyes clouded as he thought of the jangled, tangled mess that was his own parents' lives. Both his parents had married multiple times, and he had been born only seven months after their wedding—evidence they'd both been unfaithful to their previous spouses. Nor had they been faithful to each other, and his mother had walked out when he was eleven.

Both were now remarried—yet again. He'd stopped counting or caring. He'd known all along that providing their only child with a stable family was unimportant to them. Now, in his twenties, his sole purpose, or so it seemed, was to keep the Kyrgiakis coffers filled to the brim in order to fund their lavish lifestyles and expensive divorces.

With his first class degree in economics from a top university, his MBA from a world-famous business school and his keen commercial brain, this was a task that Anatole could perform more than adequately, and he knew he benefitted from it as well. Work hard, play hard—that was the motto he lived by—and he kept the toxic ties of marriage far, far away from him.

His frown deepened and his thoughts of Romola darkened. He'd hoped that her high-flying City career would stop her from having ambitions to marry him, yet here she was, like all the tedious others, thinking to make herself Mrs Anatole Kyrgiakis.

Exasperation filled him.

Why do they always want to marry me?

It was such a damn nuisance…

A dozen vehicles ahead of him he saw the traffic light turn to green. A moment later the chain of traffic was lurching forward and his foot depressed the accelerator.

And at exactly that moment a woman stepped right in front of his car…

Tia's eyes were hazed with unshed tears, her thoughts full of poor Mr Rodgers. She'd been with her ill, elderly client to the end—which had come that morning. His death had brought back all the memories of her own mother's passing, less than two years ago, when her failing hold on life had finally been severed.

Now, though, as she trudged along, lugging her ancient unwieldy suitcase, she knew she had to get to her agency before it closed for the day. She needed to be despatched to her next assignment, for as a live-in carer she had no home of her own.

She would need to cross the street to reach the agency, which was down another side street across the main road, and with the traffic so jammed from the roadworks further ahead she realised she might as well cross here. Other people were darting through the stationary traffic, which was only moving in fits and starts.

Hefting her heavy suitcase with a sudden impulse, she stepped off the pavement...

With a reaction speed he had not known he possessed, Anatole slammed down on the brake, urgently sounding his horn.

But for all his prompt action he heard the sickening thud of his car bumper impacting on something solid. Saw the woman crumple in front of his eyes.

With an oath, he hit the hazard lights then leapt from the car, stomach churning. There on the road was the woman, sunk to her knees, one hand gripping a suitcase that was all but under his bumper. The suitcase had split open, its locks crushed, and Anatole could see clothes spilling out.

The woman lifted her head, stared blankly at Anatole, apparently unaware of the danger she'd been in.

Furious words burst from him. 'What the hell did

you think you were doing? Are you a complete idiot, stepping out like that?'

Relief that the only casualty seemed to be the suitcase had flooded through Anatole, making him yell. But the woman who clearly had some kind of death wish was perfectly all right—except that as he finished yelling the blank look vanished into a storm of weeping.

Instantly his anger deflated, and he hunkered down beside the sobbing woman.

'Are you OK?' he asked.

His voice wasn't angry now, but his only answer was a renewed burst of sobbing.

Obviously not, he answered his own question.

With a heavy sigh he took the disgorged clothes, stuffed them randomly back into the suitcase, and made a futile attempt to close the lid. Then he took her arm.

'Let's get you back on the pavement safely,' he said.

He started to draw her upright. Her face lifted. Tears were pouring in an avalanche down her cheeks, and broken, breathless sobs came from her throat. But Anatole was not paying attention to her emotional outburst. As he stood her up on her feet, his brain, as if after a slow motion delay, registered two things.

The woman was younger than he'd first thought. And even weeping she was breathtakingly, jaw-droppingly lovely.

Blonde, heart-shaped face, blue-eyes, rosebud mouth...

He felt something plummet inside him, then ascend, taking shape, rearranging everything. His expression changed.

'You're all right,' he heard himself say. His voice was much gentler, with no more anger in it. 'It was a narrow escape, but you made it.'

'I'm so sorry!' The words stuttered from her as she heaved in breath chokily.

Anatole shook his head, negating her apology. 'It's all right. No harm done. Except to your suitcase.'

As she took in its broken state her face crumpled in distress. With sudden decision Anatole hefted the suitcase into the boot of his car, opened the passenger door.

'I'll drive you to wherever you're going. In you get,' he instructed, all too conscious of the traffic building up behind him, horns tooting noisily.

He propelled her into the car, despite her stammering protest. Throwing himself into his driver's seat, he turned off the hazard lights and gunned the engine.

Absently, he found himself wondering if he would have gone to so much personal inconvenience as he was now had the person who'd stepped right out in front of his car not been the breathtakingly lovely blonde that she was...

'It's no problem,' he said. 'Now, where to?'

She stared blankly. 'Um...' She cast her eyes frantically through the windscreen. 'That side street down there.'

Anatole moved off. The traffic was still crawling, and he threw his glance at his unexpected passenger. She was sniffing, wiping at her cheeks with her fingers. As the traffic halted at a red light Anatole reached for the neatly folded clean handkerchief in his jacket pocket and turned to mop at her face himself. Then he drew back, job done.

Her eyes were like saucers, widening to plates as she looked back at him. And the expression in them suddenly stilled him completely.

Slowly, very slowly, he smiled...

Tia was staring. Gawping. Her heart was thudding like a hammer, and her throat was tight from the storm of weeping triggered by the man whose car she had so blindly, stupidly, stepped in front of when he had laid into her for her carelessness. But it had been building since the grim, sad ordeal of watching an elderly, mortally ill man take his leave of life, reminding her so much of the tearing grief she'd felt at her mother's death.

Now something else was overpowering her. Her eyes were distended, and she was unable to stop staring. Staring at the man who had just mopped her face and was now sitting back in his seat, watching her staring at him with wide eyes filled with wonder...

She gulped silently, still staring disbelievingly, and words tumbled silently, chaotically in her head.

Black hair, like sable, and a face as if...as if it was carved... Eyes like dark chocolate and smoky long, long lashes. Cheekbones a mile high... And his mouth...quirking at the corner like that. I can feel my stomach hollowing out, and I don't know where to look, but I just want to go on gazing at him, because he looks exactly as if he's stepped right out of one of my daydreams... The most incredible man I've ever seen in my life...

Because how could it be otherwise? How could she possibly, in her restricted, constricted life, during which she had done nothing and seen nothing, ever have encountered a man like this?

Of course she hadn't! She'd spent her teenage years looking after her mother, and her days now were spent in caring for the sick and the elderly. There had never been opportunity or time for romantic adventures, for boyfriends, fashion, excitement. Her only romances had been in her head—woven out of time spent staring out of windows, sitting by bedsides, attending to all the chores and tasks that live-in carers had to undertake.

Except that here—right now, right here—was a man who could have sprung right out of her romantic fantasies...everything she had ever daydreamed about.

Tall, dark and impossibly handsome.

And he was here—right *here*—beside her. A daydream made real.

She gulped again. His smile deepened, indenting around his sculpted mouth, making a wash of weakness go through her again, deeper still.

'Better?' he murmured.

Silently, she nodded, still unable to tear her gaze away. Just wanting to go on gazing and gazing at him.

Then, abruptly, she became hideously aware that although *he* looked exactly as if he'd stepped out of one of her torrid daydreams—a fantasy made wondrously, amazingly real—*she* was looking no such thing. In fact the complete, mortifying opposite.

Burningly, she was brutally aware of how she must look to him—the very last image a man like him should see in any daydream, made real or not. Red eyes, snuffling nose, tear runnels down her cheeks, hair all mussed and not a scrap of make-up. Oh, yes— and she was wearing ancient jeans and a bobbled, battered jumper that hung on her body like a rag. What a disaster...

As the traffic light changed to green Anatole turned into the side street she'd indicated. 'Where now?' he asked.

It came to him that he was hoping it was some way yet. Then he crushed the thought. Picking up stray females off the street—literally, in this case!—was not a smart idea. Even though...

His glance went to her again. *She really is something to look at! Even with those red eyes and rubbish clothes.*

A thought flashed across his mind. One he didn't want but that was there all the same.

How good could she look?

Immediately he cut the thought.

No—don't ask that. Don't think that. Drive her to her destination, then drive on—back to your own life.

Yes, that was what he *should* do—he knew that perfectly well. But in the meantime he could hardly drive in silence. Besides, he didn't want her bursting into those terrifyingly heavy sobs again.

'I'm sorry you were so upset,' he heard himself saying. 'But I hope it's taught you never, *ever* to step out into traffic.'

'I'm so, *so* sorry,' she said again. Her voice was husky now. 'And I'm so, *so* sorry for...for crying like that. It wasn't you! Well, I mean...not really. Only when you yelled at me—'

'It was shock,' Anatole said. 'I was terrified I'd killed you.' He threw a rueful look at her. 'I didn't mean to make you cry.'

She shook her head. 'It wasn't because of that—not really,' she said again. 'It was because—'

She stopped. All thoughts of daydream heroes vanished as the memory of how she'd spent the night at the bedside of a dying man assailed her again.

'Because…?' Anatole prompted, throwing her another brief glance. He found he liked throwing her glances. But that he would have preferred them not to be brief…

Perhaps they need not be—

She was answering him, cutting across the thought he should not have. Most *definitely* should not have.

'It was because of poor Mr Rodgers!' she said in a rush. 'He died this morning. I was there. I was his care worker. It was so sad. He was very old, but all the same—' She broke off, a catch in her voice. 'It reminded me of when my mother died—'

She broke off again, and Anatole could hear the half-sob in her voice. 'I'm sorry,' he said, because it seemed the only thing to say. 'Was your mother's death recent?'

She shook her head. 'No, it was nearly two years ago, but it brought it all back. She had MS—all the time I was growing up, really—and after my father was killed I looked after her. That's why I became a care worker. I had the experience, and anyway there wasn't much else I could do, and a live-in post was essential because I don't have a place of my own yet—'

She broke off, suddenly horribly aware that she was saying all these personal things to a complete stranger.

She swallowed. 'I'm just going to my agency's offices now—to get a new assignment, somewhere to go tonight.' Her voice changed. 'That's it—just there!'

She pointed to an unprepossessing office block and Anatole drew up alongside it. She got out, tried the front door. It did not open. He stepped out beside her, seeing the notice that said 'Closed'.

'What now?' he heard himself saying in a tight voice.

Tia turned to stare at him, trying to mask the dismay in her face. 'Oh, I'll find a cheap hotel for tonight. There's probably one close by I can walk to.'

Anatole doubted that—especially with her broken suitcase.

His eyes rested on her. She looked lost and helpless. And very, very lovely.

As before, sudden decision took him. There was a voice in his head telling him he was mad, behaving like an idiot, but he ignored it. Instead, he smiled suddenly.

'I've got a much better idea,' he said. 'Look, you can't move that broken suitcase a metre, let alone trail around looking for a mythical cheap hotel in London! So here's what I propose. Why not stay the night at my flat? I won't be there,' he added immediately, because instantly panic had filled her blue eyes, 'so you'll have the run of it. Then you can buy yourself a new suitcase in the morning and head to your agency.' He smiled. 'How would that be?'

She was staring at him as though she dared not believe what he was saying. 'Are you sure?' That disbelief was in her voice, but her panic was ebbing away.

'I wouldn't offer otherwise,' Anatole replied.

'It's incredibly kind of you,' she answered, her voice sounding husky, her eyes dropping away from his. 'I'm being a total pain to you—'

'Not at all,' he said. 'So, do you accept?'

He smiled again—the deliberate smile that he

used when he wanted people to do what he wanted. It worked this time too. Tremulously she nodded.

Refusing to pay any attention to the voice in his head telling him he was an insane idiot to make such an offer to a complete stranger, however lovely, Anatole helped her back into the car and set off again, heading into Mayfair, where his flat was.

He glanced at her. She was sitting very still, hands in her lap, looking out through the windscreen, not at him. She still looked as if she could not believe this was really happening.

He took the next step in making it real for her. For him as well.

'Maybe we should introduce ourselves properly? I'm Anatole Kyrgiakis.'

It was odd to say his own name, because he usually didn't have to, and certainly when he did he expected his surname, at least, to be recognised instantly. Possibly followed by a quick glance to ascertain that he meant *the* Kyrgiakis family. This time, however, his name drew no reaction other than her turning her head to look at him as he spoke.

'Tia Saunders,' she responded shyly.

'Hello, Tia,' Anatole said in a low voice, with a flickering smile.

He saw a flush of colour in her cheeks, then had to pay attention to the traffic again. He let her be as he drove on, needing to concentrate now and wanting her to feel a little more relaxed about what was happening. But she was still clearly tense as he pulled up outside his elegant Georgian town house and guided her indoors, carrying her broken suitcase.

The greeting from the concierge at the desk in the

wide hallway seemed to make her shrink against him, and as they entered his top-floor apartment she gave a gasp.

'I can't stay here!' she exclaimed, dismay in her voice. 'I might mess something up!'

Her eyes raced around, taking in a long white sofa, covered in silk cushions, a thick dove-grey carpet that matched the lavish drapes at the wide windows. It was like something out of a movie—absolutely immaculate and obviously incredibly expensive.

Anatole gave a laugh. 'Just don't spill coffee on anything,' he said.

She shook her head violently. 'Please, don't even *say* that!' she cried, aghast at the very thought.

His expression changed. She seemed genuinely worried. He walked up to her. Found himself taking her hand with his free one even without realising it. Patting it reassuringly.

'Speaking of coffee… I could murder a cup! What about you?'

She nodded, swallowing. 'Th…thank you,' she stammered.

'Good. I'll get the machine going. But let me show you to your room first—and, look, why not take a shower, freshen up? You must have had a gruelling night, from what you've said.'

He relinquished her hand, hefted up the broken suitcase again, mentally deciding he'd get a new one delivered by the concierge within the hour, and carried it through to one of the guest bedrooms.

She followed after him, still glancing about her with an air of combined nervousness and wide-eyed amazement at her surroundings, as if she'd never seen anything like it in her life. Which, he realised, she probably never had.

An unusual sense of satisfaction darted within him. It was a good feeling to give this impoverished, waiflike girl, who'd clearly had a pretty sad time of it—both parents dead and a poorly paid job involving distressing end-of-life care—a brief taste of luxury. He found himself wanting her to enjoy it.

Setting down the suitcase, which immediately sprang open again, he pointed out the en suite bathroom, then with another smile left her to it, heading for the kitchen.

Five minutes later the coffee was brewing and he was sprawled on the sofa, checking his emails—trying very, very hard not to let his mind wander to his unexpected guest taking her shower...

He wondered just how far her charms extended beyond her lovely face. He suspected a lot further. She was slender—he'd seen that instantly—but it hadn't made her flat-chested. No, indeed, Even though she was wearing cheap, unflattering clothes, he'd seen the soft swell of her breasts beneath. And she was petite—much more so than the women he usually selected for himself.

Maybe that was because of his own height—over six foot—or maybe it was because the kind of women he went out with tended to be self-assured, self-confident high-achieving females who were his counterparts in many ways, striding through the world knowing their own worth, very sure of themselves and their attractions.

Women like Romola.

His expression changed. Before Tia had plunged in

front of his car he'd made the decision to cut Romola out of his life—so why not do that right now? He'd text her to say he couldn't see her tonight after all, that something had come up, and that it was unlikely he'd be back in London any time soon, Say that perhaps they should both accept their time together had run its course…

With a ruthlessness that he could easily exercise whenever he felt himself targeted by a woman wanting more of him than he cared to give, he sent the text, softening the blow with the despatch of a diamond bracelet as a farewell gift as a sop to Romola's considerable ego. Then, with a sense of relief, he turned his thoughts back to tonight.

A smile started around his mouth, his eyes softening slightly. He'd already played out King Cophetua and the Beggar Maid in offering Tia the run of his flat, so why not go the whole hog and give her an evening she would always remember? Champagne, fine dining—the works!

It was something he'd take a bet that she'd never experienced in her deprived life before.

Of course it went without saying that that would be *all* he'd be offering her. He himself would not be staying here—he'd make his way over to the Mayfair hotel where his father kept a permanent suite. Of course he would.

Anything else was completely out of the question—however lovely she was.

Completely out, he told himself sternly.

CHAPTER TWO

TIA STOOD IN a state of physical bliss as the hot water poured over her body, foaming into rich suds the shampoo and body wash she'd found in the basket of expensive-looking toiletries on the marble-topped vanity unit. Never in her whole life had she had such a lavish, luxurious shower.

By the time she stepped out, her hair wrapped up in a fleecy towel, another huge bath sheet wrapped around her, she felt reborn. She still hadn't really got her head around what was happening because it all just seemed like a fairytale—swept off by a prince who took her breath away.

He's just so gorgeous! So incredibly gorgeous! And he's being so kind! He could just as easily have left me on the pavement with my broken suitcase. Driven away and not cared!

But he hadn't driven away—he'd brought her here, and how could she possibly have said no? In all her confined, unexciting life, dedicated to caring for her poor mother and for others, when had anything like this *ever* happened except in her daydreams?

She lifted her chin, staring at her reflection, resolve

in her eyes. Whatever was happening, she was going to seize this moment!

She whirled about, yanking off the turban towel, letting her damp hair tumble down, then rapidly sorting through her clothes, desperate to find something—anything—that was more worthy of the occasion than her ancient jeans and baggy top. Of course she had nothing at all that was remotely suitable, but at least she had something that was an improvement. She might never hope to be able to look like a fairytale princess, but she'd do her damnedest!

As she walked back into that pristine, palatial lounge her eyes went straight to the darkly sprawling figure relaxed on the white sofa. Dear Lord, but he was unutterably gorgeous!

He'd shed his formal business jacket and loosened his tie, undone his top button and turned up his cuffs. And through her veins came that same devastating rush she'd felt before, weakening her limbs, making her dizzy with its impact.

He rose to his feet. 'There you are.' He smiled. 'Come and sit down and have your coffee.'

He nodded to where he'd set out a plate of pastries, extracted from the freezer and microwaved by his own fair hand into tempting, fragrant warmth. Two had already been consumed, but there were plenty left.

'Are you on a diet?' he asked convivially. 'Or can I tempt you?'

Anatole watched with a sense of familiarity as the colour rushed into her face and then out again. Maybe he shouldn't have used the word 'tempt'. He had the damnedest feeling that it wasn't the thought of the pastries that were making her colour up like that.

Snap!

Because if *she* was experiencing temptation, then he knew for sure that he was as well. And with good reason...

She'd changed her clothes and, although they were still clearly cheap and high street, they were a definite improvement. She'd put on a skirt—a floaty cotton one, in Indian print—and topped it with a turquoise tee shirt that gave her a whole lot more figure than the baggy jumper she'd had on previously. On top of that, her freshly washed hair was loose now, still damp, but curling in a tousled mane around her shoulders. The redness had finally gone from her eyes, and her skin was clear and unblemished. Her lips rosy, tender...

Still the ingénue, definitely...but no longer a sad waif.

With an expression of intense self-consciousness on her face, she gingerly sat herself down on the sofa, slanting her slender legs. He saw her hands were shaking slightly as she took the coffee he'd poured with a low murmur of thanks.

She drank it thirstily, hoping it would steady her wildly jangling nerves, and her eyes jumped again to Anatole to drink in the gorgeous reality of his presence. Her eyes met his and she realised he was watching her, a smile playing around his mouth. It was a smile that sent little quivers shimmering through her and made her breath shallow.

'Have a pastry,' he said, pushing the plate towards her.

Their warm, yeasty cinnamon scent caught at her, reminding her that she'd not had a chance to eat all day. She took one, grabbing a thick, richly patterned

paper napkin as she did so, terrified of dropping but-
tery flakes on the pristine upholstery or the carpet.

Anatole watched her polish off the pastry, letting
his eyes drift over the sweet perfection of her heart-
shaped face, the cerulean eyes, the delicate arch of her
brows, the soft curls of her fair hair.

*She is breathtakingly lovely—and she is taking my
breath away just looking at her...*

He glanced at his watch. It was coming up to seven,
though the evenings were still light. They could drink
champagne on his roof terrace. But first...best to order
dinner.

He reached for his laptop, brought up the website
for the service he used when dining in, then tilted the
screen towards her. 'Take a look,' he invited, 'and
see what you'd like for dinner. I'm going to order in.'

Immediately—predictably—she shook her head.
'Oh, no, please—not for me. I'm absolutely fine just
eating these pastries.'

'Yes, well, I'm not,' he rejoined affably. 'Come
on—take a look. What sort of food do you like best?
And do *not*,' he added sternly, 'say pizza! Or Indian.
Or Chinese. I'm talking gourmet food here—take your
pick.'

Wide-eyed, Tia stared at the long page of menu options on the screen. She couldn't understand most of
them. She swallowed.

'Will you let me choose for you?' Anatole asked,
realising her dilemma.

She nodded gratefully.

'Anything you're allergic to?' he asked.

She shook her head, but all the same he chose rel-
atively safe options—no shellfish, no nuts. A mid-

night dash to A&E was *not* the way he wanted this evening to end.

And you're not going to let it end the way you're thinking right now either! his conscience admonished him sternly.

Not even when he was leaning towards her, and she towards him, so they could both read the screen, and he could catch the fresh scent of her body. All he would have to do to touch her would be to lift his hand, let it slide through those softly drying curls, splay his fingers around the nape of her neck and draw that sweet, tender mouth to his...

He straightened abruptly, busying himself with putting the order through, then closing his laptop. Time to fetch the champagne.

He returned a few moments later, with a bottle at the perfect temperature from his thermostatically controlled wine store and two flutes dangling from his hand. He crossed to the picture window, sliding it open.

'Come and see the view,' he said invitingly.

Tia got to her feet, following him out on to a roofline terrace with a stone balustrade along it. She was still in a daze. Was he really intending to have dinner with her? Drink champagne with her? Her heart was beating faster, she knew, just at the very thought of it.

As she stepped out the warm evening air enveloped her. Sunshine was still catching the tops of the trees visible in the park beyond. Nor was that the only greenery visible—copious large stone pots adorned the terrace, lush with plants, creating a little oasis.

'Oh, it's so lovely!' she exclaimed spontaneously, her face lighting up.

Anatole smiled, feeling a kick go through him at her visible pleasure, at how it made her eyes shine, and set down the champagne and flutes on a little ironwork table flanked by two chairs.

'A private green haven,' he said. 'Cities aren't my favourite places, so when I'm forced to be in them—which is all too often, alas—I like to be as green as I can. It's one of the reasons,' he went on, 'that I like penthouse apartments—they come with roof terraces.'

He paused to open the champagne with a soft pop of the cork, then handed her one of the empty flutes.

'Keep it slightly tilted,' he instructed as he poured it half full, letting the liquid foam, but not too much. Then he filled his own glass and lifted it to her, looking down at her. She really was petite, he found himself thinking again. And for some reason it made him feel…protective.

It was an odd thought. Unfamiliar to him when it came to women.

He smiled down at her. She was gazing up at him, and the expression in her eyes sent that kick through him again. He lifted his glass, indicating that she should do the same, which she did, glancing at the foaming liquid as if she could not believe it was in her hand.

'*Yammas,*' he said.

She looked confused.

'It's *cheers* in Greek,' he elucidated.

'Oh,' she said, '*that's* what you are! I knew you must be foreign, because of your name, but I didn't know what—'

She coloured. Had she sounded rude? She hadn't meant to. London was incredibly multicultural—there had been no reason to say he was 'foreign'. He was probably as British as she was—

'I'm sorry,' she said, looking dismayed. 'I didn't mean to imply—'

'No,' he said, reassuringly. 'I *am* foreign. I'm a Greek national. But I do a lot of work in London because it's a major financial hub. I live in Greece, though.' He smiled again, wanting to set her at her ease. 'Have you ever been to Greece? For a holiday, maybe?'

Tia shook her head. 'We went to Spain when I was little,' she said. 'When my dad was still alive and before mum got MS.' She swallowed, looking away.

'It's good to have memories,' Anatole said quietly. 'Especially of family holidays as a child.'

Yes—it *was* good to have such memories. Except he didn't have any. His school holidays—breaks from boarding at the exclusive international school in Switzerland he'd attended from the age of seven—had been spent either at friends' houses or rattling around the huge Kyrgiakis mansion in Athens, with no one except the servants around.

His parents had been busy with their own more important lives.

When he'd reached his teens he'd taken to spending a few weeks with his uncle—his father's older brother. Vasilis had never been interested in business or finance. He was a scholar, content to bury himself in libraries and museums, using the Kyrgiakis money to fund archaeological research and sponsor the arts. He disapproved of his younger brother's amatory dissoluteness, but never criticised him openly. He was a lifelong bachelor, and Anatole had found him kindly, but remote—though very helpful in coaching him in exam revision and for university entrance.

Anatole had come to value him increasingly for his wise, quiet good sense.

He cleared his thoughts. 'Well, here's to your first trip to Greece—which I'm sure you'll make one day.' He smiled, tilting his glass again at Tia, then taking a mouthful of the softly beading champagne. He watched her do likewise, very tentatively, as if she could not believe she was doing so.

'Is this real champagne?' she asked as she lowered her glass again.

Anatole's mouth twitched. 'Definitely,' he assured her. 'Do you like it?'

And suddenly, out of nowhere, a huge smile split her face, transforming the wary nervousness of her expression. 'It's gorgeous!' she exclaimed.

Just like you are!

Those were the words blazing in her head, as she gazed at the man who was standing there, who had scooped up the crumpled heap she'd made on the road and brought her here, to this beautiful apartment, to drink champagne—the first champagne she'd ever tasted.

Should I pinch myself? Is this real—is this really, really real?

She wanted it to be—oh, how she wanted it to be! But she could scarcely believe it.

Maybe the single mouthful of champagne had made her bold. 'This is so incredibly kind of you!' she said in a rush.

Kind? The word resonated in Anatole's head. *Was*

he being kind? He'd told himself he was, but was the truth different?

Am I just being incredibly, recklessly self-indulgent?

He lifted his glass again. Right now he didn't care. His only focus was on this lovely woman—so young, so fresh, so breathtakingly captivating in her simple natural beauty.

She is practising no arts to attract me, making no eyes at me, and she asks nothing of me—

He smiled, his expression softening, a tinge of humour at his mouth. 'Drink up,' he said, 'we've a whole bottle to get through!'

He took another mouthful of the fine vintage, encouraging her to do likewise.

She was looking around her as she sipped, out over the rooftops of the houses nearby. 'It's nice to think,' she heard herself say, 'that even though up here used to be the attics, where the servants lived, they got this view!'

Anatole laughed. 'Well, the attics have certainly gone up in the world since then!' he answered, thinking of the multi-million-pound price tag this apartment had come with. 'And it's good that those days are gone. Any house staff these days get a lot better than attics to live in, and they are very decently paid.'

Probably, he found himself adding silently, *a lot more than you get as a care worker...*

He frowned. Essential though such work was, surely it would be good if she aspired to something more in her life?

'Tell me,' he said, taking some more of his champagne, then topping up both their glasses, 'what do you want to do with your life? I know care work is important, but surely you won't want to do it for ever?'

Even as he asked the question it dawned on him that never in his life had he come across anyone from her background. All the women he knew were either in high-powered careers or trust fund princesses. Completely a different species from this young woman with her sad, impoverished, hard-working life.

Tia bit her lip, feeling awkward suddenly. 'Well, because I was off school a lot, looking after Mum, I never passed my exams, so I can't really go to college. And, though I'm saving from my wages, I can't afford accommodation of my own yet.'

'Have you no family at all to help you?' Anatole frowned.

She shook her head. 'It was just Dad, Mum, and me.'

She looked at him. Nearly a glass down on the champagne and she was definitely feeling bold. This might be a daydream, but she was going to indulge herself to the hilt with it.

'What about you?' she asked. 'Aren't Greek families huge?'

Anatole gave a thin smile. 'Not mine,' he said tersely. 'I'm an only child too.' He looked into his champagne flute. 'My parents are divorced, and both of them are married to other people now. I don't see much of them.'

That was from choice. His and theirs. The only regular Kyrgiakis family gathering was the annual board meeting when all the shareholders gathered— himself, his parents and his uncle, and a few distant cousins as well. All of them looked to him to find out how much more money he'd poured into the family coffers, thanks to his business acumen.

'Oh,' Tia said, sympathetically, 'that's a shame.'

An unwelcome flicker went through her. She didn't want to think that fantasy males like this one could have dysfunctional families like ordinary people. Surely when they lived in fantastic, deluxe places like this, and drank vintage champagne, they couldn't have problems like other people?

Anatole gave another thin smile. 'Not particularly,' he countered. 'I'm used to it.'

Absently, he wondered why he'd talked about his family at all. He never did that with women. He glanced at his watch. They should go indoors. Dinner would be arriving shortly and he didn't want to think about his family—or his lack of any that he bothered about. Even Vasilis, kindly though he was, lived in a world of his own, content with his books and his philanthropic activities in the arts world.

He guided his guest indoors. Dusk was gathering outside and he switched on the terrace lighting, casting low pools of soft light around the greenery, giving it an elvish glow.

Once again, Tia was enchanted. 'Oh, that's so pretty!' she exclaimed, as the effect sprang to life. 'It looks like a fairyland!'

She immediately felt childish saying such a thing, even if it were true, but Anatole laughed, clearly amused.

The house phone rang, alerting him that dinner was on its way up, and five minutes later he and Tia were seated, tucking in to their first course—a delicate white fish terrine.

'This is delicious!' she exclaimed, her face lighting up as she ate.

She said the same thing about the chicken bathed in a creamy sauce, with tiny new potatoes and fresh green beans—simple, but beautifully cooked.

Anatole smiled indulgently. 'Eat up,' he urged.

It was good to see a woman eating with appetite, not picking at her food. Good, too, to see the open pleasure in her face at dining with him, her appreciation of everything. Including the champagne as he topped up her glass yet again.

Careful. He heard the warning voice in his head. *Don't give her more than she can handle.*

Or, indeed, more than he could handle either—not when he still had to get to the hotel for the night. But that wasn't yet, and for now he could continue to enjoy every moment of their evening.

A sense of well-being settled over him. Deliberately, he kept the conversation between them light, doing most of the talking himself, but drawing her out as well, intent on making her feel relaxed and comfortable.

'If you do ever manage to get to Greece for a holiday, what kind of thing would you most like doing? Are you a beach bunny or do you like sightseeing? There's plenty of both across the mainland and the islands. And if you like ancient history there's no better place in the world than Greece, to my mind!' he said lightly.

'I don't really know anything about ancient history,' she answered, colouring slightly.

She felt uncomfortable, being reminded of her lack of education. Such realities got in the way of this wonderful, blissful daydream she was having. This real-life fairytale.

'You've heard of the Parthenon?' Anatole prompted.

A look of confusion passed over Tia's face. 'Um… is it a temple?'

'Yes, the most famous in the world—on the Acropolis in Athens. A lot of tall stone pillars around a rectangular ruin.'

'Oh, yes, I've seen pictures!' she acknowledged, relieved that she'd been right.

'Well, there you are, then.' He smiled, and went on to tell her the kind of information most tourists gathered from a visit to the site, then moved on to the other attractions that his homeland offered.

Whether or not she took it all in, he didn't know. Mostly she just gazed at him, her beautiful blue eyes wide—something he found himself enjoying. Especially when he held her gaze and saw the flush of colour mount in her cheeks, her hand reaching hurriedly for the glass of iced water beside her champagne flute.

As they moved on to the final course—a light-as-air pavlova—he opened a bottle of sweet dessert wine, calculating that she would find it more palatable than port.

Which, indeed, she did, sipping the honeyed liquid with appreciation.

When all the pavlova was gone, Anatole got to his feet. He'd set coffee to brew when he'd fetched the dessert wine, and now he collected it, setting it down on the coffee table by the sofa.

He held his hand out to Tia. 'Come and sit down,' he invited.

She got up from the table, suddenly aware that her

head was feeling as if there was a very slight swirl inside it. Just how much of that gorgeous champagne had she drunk? she wondered. It seemed to be fizzing in her veins, making her feel breathless, weightless. As if she were floating in a blissful haze. But she didn't care. How could she? An evening like this—something out of fairyland—would never come again!

With a little contented sigh she sank down on the sofa, the dessert wine glass in her hand, her light cotton skirt billowing around her.

Anatole came and sat down beside her. 'Time to relax,' he said genially, flicking on the TV with a remote.

He hefted his feet up onto the coffee table, disposing of his tie over the back of the sofa. He wanted to be totally comfortable. The mix of champagne and sweet wine was creaming pleasantly in his veins. He hoped it was doing so in Tia, as well, allowing her to enjoy the rest of the evening with him before he took himself off to his hotel.

Idly, he wondered whether he should phone and tell them to expect him, but then he decided not to bother. Instead he amused himself by channel-surfing until he chanced upon a channel that made his unexpected guest exclaim, 'Oh, I *love* this movie!'

It was a rom-com, perfectly watchable, and he was happy to do so. Happy to see Tia curl her bare feet under her skirt on the sofa and lean back into the cushions, her eyes on the screen.

At what point, Anatole wondered as he topped up her glass again, had he moved closer to her? At what point, as he'd stretched and flexed his legs, had he also stretched and flexed his arms, so that one of them was now resting along the back of the sofa, his fingertips grazing the top of her shoulder?

At what point had his fingers started idly playing with the now dry silky-soft pale curls around her neck?

At what point had he accepted that he had no desire—none whatsoever—to go anywhere else tonight?

And all the caution and the warnings sounding in his head, in what remained of his conscience, were falling on ears that were totally, profoundly deaf...

The film came to its sentimental end, with the hero sweeping the heroine up into his arms, lavishing an extravagant kiss upon her upturned face, and the music soared into the credits. A huge sigh of satisfaction was breathed from Tia, and she set down her now empty glass, turning back towards Anatole.

Emotion was coursing through her, mingling with the champagne and with that deliciously sweet wine she'd been drinking, with the gorgeous food she'd eaten—the best she'd ever tasted—all set off by candles and soft music and with her very own prince to keep her company.

It was foaming in her bloodstream, shining from her eyes. The rom-com they'd watched was one of her favourites, sighed over many times, but this— this now, *here*, right now—with her very own gorgeous, incredibly handsome man sitting beside her, oh, so tantalisingly close, was *real*! No fairytale, no fantasy—*real*. She'd never been this physically close to a man before—let alone a man like this! A man who could make fairytales come true...

And she knew how fairytales culminated! With the hero kissing the heroine...

Excitement, wonder—*hope*—filled her, and her eyes were shining like stars as she gazed up into the face of this glorious, gorgeous man who represented to her everything she had ever longed for, dreamt of, yearned for.

The man who was looking down at her, his dark eyes lustrous, his lashes long and lush, his sculpted mouth so beautiful, so sensual—

She felt a little thrill just thinking of it, her breath catching, her eyes widening as she looked up to his.

Anatole looked down at her, seeing the loveliness of her face, of the loose, long pale hair waving like silk over her slender shoulders, seeing how the sweet mounds of her breasts were pressed against the contours of her cotton tee shirt, how her soft tender lips were parted, how her celestial blue eyes were wide, gazing at him with an expression that told him exactly what she wanted.

For one long, endless moment he stayed motionless, while a million conflicting thoughts battled in his head over what he should do next. What he *should* do versus what he wanted to do.

Yet still he held back, knowing that what he wanted so badly to do he should not. He should instead pull back, make some gesture of withdrawal from her, get up, get to his feet, increase the distance between them. Because if he didn't right now, then—

Her hand lifted, almost quivering, and with trembling fingers she let the delicate tips touch his jaw, feather-light, scarcely making contact, as if she hardly dared believe that this was what she was doing. She said his name. Breathed it. Her eyes were pools of longing. Her lips were parted, eyes half closed now. Waiting—yearning... For him.

And Anatole lost it. Lost all remaining shreds of conscience or consciousness.

He leaned towards her. The hand behind her head grazed her nape, his other hand slid along her cheek, his fingers gentle in her hair, cupping her face. Her eyes were wide, like saucers, and in them starlight shone like beacons, drawing him into her, into doing what she so blazingly wanted him to do.

His eyes washed over her, his pulse quickening. She was so lovely. And she so wanted him to kiss her... He could see it in her eyes, in her parted lips, in the quivering pulse in her delicate white throat.

His lashes swept down over his eyes as his mouth touched hers, soft as velvet, tasting the sweet wine on her lips, the warmth of her mouth as he opened it to his questing silken touch. He heard her give a little moan, deep in her throat, and he felt his own pulse surge, arousal spearing within him.

She was so soft to kiss, and he deepened his kiss automatically, instinctively, his hand sliding down over the curve of her shoulder, turning her towards him as he leant into her, drawing her to him, drawing her across him, so that her hand now braced itself against the hard wall of his chest, so that one slender thigh was against his.

He heard her moan again and it quickened his arousal. He said her name, told her how sweet she was, how very lovely. If he spoke in Greek he didn't realise it—didn't realise anything except that the wine was coursing in his bloodstream, recklessness was heady in his smitten synapses, and in his arms was a woman he desired.

Who desired him.

Because that was what her tender, lissom body was telling him—that was what the sudden engorgement of her breasts was showing him in the cresting of her nipples that were somehow beneath the palm of his hand.

Without realisation, she was winding her hand around his waist. He laid her back across his lap, half supported on his arm as he kissed her still, one hand palming her swelling breast until she moaned, eyes closed, her face filled with an expression of bliss he would have had to be blind not to see. He lifted his mouth from hers, let his eyes feast on her a moment, before his mouth descended yet again to graze on the line of her cheekbones, to nip at the tender lobes of her ears.

He let his hand slip reluctantly from her breast and then slide languorously along her flank to rest on her thigh, to smooth away the light cotton of her skirt until his hand found the bare skin beneath. To stroke and to caress and to hear her moan again, to feel her thigh strain against him—feel, too, his own body surge to full arousal.

Desire flamed in him…strong, impossible to resist…

And yet he *must*. This was too fast, too intense. He was letting his overpowering desire for her carry him away and he must draw back.

Heart pounding, he set her aside.

'Tia—' His voice was broken, his hand raised as if to ward her off. To hold himself back from her.

He saw her face fill with anguish. It caught at him like a blow.

'Don't…don't you want me?' There was dismay in her voice, which was a muted whisper.

He gave a groan. 'Tia—I mustn't. This isn't right. I can't take advantage of you like this!'

Immediately she cried out, 'But you aren't! Oh, please, *please* don't tell me you don't want me! I couldn't bear it!'

Her hand flew to her mouth and her look of anguish intensified. Her breathing was fast and breathless and she felt bereft—lost and abandoned.

He caught her face between his hands. 'Tia—I want you very, very much, but—'

But there's more than one bedroom in this apartment and we have to be in separate bedrooms tonight—we just have to be! Because anything else would be…would be…

Her face had lit like a beacon again. 'Please… *please*!' she begged. Her face worked. 'This whole evening with you has been incredible! Fantastic! Wonderful! And now…with you…it's like nothing I've ever experienced in all my life! You are like no one I've ever met! I'll never meet anyone else like you again, and this…all this…'

She gestured at the room, softly lit with table lamps, at the candles still on the dining table, the empty bottle of champagne, the glow of the lights on the terrace beyond.

'All this will never happen to me again!' She bit her lip, mouth quivering. 'I want this *so* much,' she said huskily, her eyes pleading with him, her hand fastening on his strong arm as if she might draw him back to her again. *'Please,'* she begged again. 'Please don't turn me away—*please*!'

And yet again Anatole lost it.

Unable to resist what he did not want to resist, what he could not bear to resist, he swept her back up to him, his mouth descending to taste again the honeyed sweetness of her mouth which opened to his instantly, eagerly…hungrily.

She wants this—she wants this as much as I do. And, however briefly we have known each other, my desire for her is overpowering. And so is hers for me. And because of that…

Because of that, with a rasp deep in his throat, he hefted to his feet, holding her in his arms, his hand sweeping under her knees to cradle her against him as he carried her away.

Away not to the guest room but to his own master suite, where he ripped back the bedcovers to lay her gently upon cool sheets. She was gazing up at him, blindness in her eyes, her pupils flared, lips beestung, breasts straining against the moulding of the cotton tee.

He wanted it gone. Wanted all her clothes gone, and all his—wanted no barriers between himself and this lovely woman he wanted now…*right* now…

CHAPTER THREE

TIA GAZED UP at him—at this incredible, unbearably devastating man—her mind in whiteout. Her body seemed to be on fire, with a soft, velvet flame, glowing with a sensual awareness that was possessing her utterly. She reached her arms up to him, yearning for him, beseeching him to take her back in his arms, to kiss and caress her, to sweep her off into the gorgeous bliss of his touch, his desire for her.

He was stripping off his clothes and she could feel her eyes widen as his shirt revealed the smooth, taut contours of his chest. And then his fingers were at his belt, snaking it free...

She gave a little cry, turning her head into the pillow, suddenly desperately shy. She had never dreamt that a man like this would ever be real in her life, and he was suddenly only too real.

Then she felt the mattress dip, felt his weight coming down beside her, heard him murmur soft words, urgent words, seductive, irresistible...and then his hand was curving her face back towards his, and he was so close to her, so very close, and in his eyes was a light she had never seen in a man's eyes before. She'd never seen a man's eyes so filled with blazing, burning fire...

I can't stop this—I can't stop it—and I don't want to! Oh, I don't want to!

She wanted it to happen, wanted what would happen now—what must happen now—wanted it with all her being, yearned and longed for it. It had come out of nowhere—just as the whole encounter with this amazing, fabulous man had come out of nowhere.

And I can't say no to it. I can't and I don't want to. I want to say yes—only yes....

Her eyes fluttered closed and she felt his mouth feather-light on hers, like swansdown. She felt his hands move to her waist, lift the material of her tee shirt from her, easing it over her head with hardly a pause in his sweet kissing. She felt his hands—warm, strong, skilled—slide around her back, unfasten her bra and slip it from her, discarding it somewhere. She knew not where and she did not care—did not care at all except that now he was doing the same with her skirt, skimming it from her, and then... Oh, then he was easing her panties from her quickening thighs.

He lifted himself from her, one hand splaying into her hair as it spread in tumbling golden curls across the pillow. His eyes burned into hers. 'You are so, so beautiful,' he said. 'So beautiful...'

She could say nothing, could only gaze upwards, hearing her mind echoing his words... *He* was beautiful! He with his sable hair and his sculpted cheekbones, with eyes you could drown in. His hard, lean body that her hands were now lifting themselves to of their own accord.

Her fingertips traced every line, every contour of the smooth, honed muscles. He seemed to shudder and she felt his muscles clench, as if what she was doing was unbearable, and then his mouth descended again.

Hungry…oh, so hungry.

And there was a hunger in her too. A ravening hunger that was as instinctive, as overpowering, as her need to be held and kissed and caressed by this most blissfully seductive of men. It was making her body arch to his, the blood rush like a torrent in her veins, drowning her senses, turning her into living flame. Never had she imagined that passion could feel like this! Never had her daydreams known what it was to be like this, in the arms of a man filled with urgent desire.

And she desired him.

She clung to him, not knowing what she was doing, only that it was what she burned to do. Her body arched to his, her thighs parting. She heard him say something but was lost to all coherence.

He seemed to pause, pull away from her, and it was unbearable not to have his warm, strong body over hers. And then, with a rush of relief, she felt him there again, kissing her again, his hands urgent, every muscle in his body tautening. She felt his body ease between hers, felt his hips move against hers, felt—

Pain! A sudden, piercing stab of pain!

She cried out, freezing, and he froze too. He gazed down at her, his eyes blind, then clearing into vision. Words escaped him. He was shocked.

He lifted from her and the pain vanished. Her hands reached for him, her head lifting blindly to catch his mouth again. But he was still withdrawn from her.

'I didn't know—I didn't realise—' The words fell from him. Shocked. Abrupt.

She could only gaze up at him. Devastation was flooding through her.

'Don't you want me?' It was all that was in her head now—the devastation of his rejection before.

'Tia...' He said her name again. 'I didn't realise that I would be the first man for you—'

Her hands pressed into his bare shoulders. 'I *want* you to be! Only you! Please—oh, *please*!'

Conflict seared in him. He burned for her, and yet—

But she was pressing her body against his, crushing her breasts against the wall of his chest. Lifting her hips to his in an age-old invitation of woman to man, to possess and be possessed.

'Please...' she said, her voice a low husk, a plea. 'Please—I want this so much—I want *you* so much.'

Her hand slid around the base of his skull, pressing against it, drawing his head down. She reached up with her mouth, feeling as her lips touched his a relief go through her that sated all her ardent yearning, all her desperate desire.

She opened his mouth under hers and Anatole, with a low, helpless groan, abandoned all his inner conflict, let himself yield to what he so wanted to do... to make her his.

It was morning. The undrawn curtains were letting in the light of dawn. Drowsily, wonderingly, Tia lay in Anatole's arms. There had been no more pain, and he had been as gentle with her as if she were made of porcelain—though the soft tenderness of her body now proclaimed that she was flesh and blood. But there was only a fading ache now, and in the cocoon of his strong arms it mattered not at all.

His arm was beneath her shoulder, her head lax upon it, and she smiled up at him, bemused, enchanted. His dark eyes were moving over her face, his other hand smoothing the tendrils of her silken hair from her cheeks. He was smiling back at her—a smile of intimacy, endearment. It made her feel weak with longing.

Bliss enveloped her, and a wonder so great that she could scarcely dare to believe that it was true, what had happened.

'Do you *have* to return to work?' Anatole was asking her.

She frowned a little, not understanding. 'The agency will open again at nine,' she said.

Anatole shook her head. 'I mean, do you have to take up another position? Are you booked to be a carer for someone else?'

Her frown deepened. She was understanding even less.

He smoothed her silken hair again, his eyes searching her face. 'I don't want you to go,' he said to her. 'I want you to stay with me.'

He watched her expression change. Watched it transform before his very eyes. Saw her cerulean blue eyes widen as she took in the meaning of what he'd said.

His smile deepened. Became assured. 'I have to go to Athens this week. Come with me—'

Come with me.

The words echoed in his head. He was sure of them—absolutely, totally sure. He felt a wash of de-

sire go through him—not for consummation but for
continuation.

*I don't want to let her go—I want to keep her with
me.*

The realisation was absolute. The clarity of his desire incontrovertible.

'Do you mean it?'

Her words were so faint he could hardly hear them.
But he could hear the emotion in her voice, see how
her expression had changed, how her eyes were flar-
ing wide, and in them hope blazed, dimmed only by
confusion.

He brushed her parted lips. 'I would not ask you
otherwise,' he said, knowing that to be true.

His arm around her tightened. She was so soft in
his arms, so tiny, it seemed to him, nestling up against
him.

He smiled at her. 'Well?' he asked. 'Will you come
with me?'

The shadow of confusion, of fear that she had mis-
understood, that he did not really mean what he'd said,
vanished. Like the sun coming out, her smile lit up
her face.

'Oh, yes! Yes, yes, *yes!*'

He laughed. He had had no fear that she would say
no—why should she? The night they had spent together had been wondrous for her—he knew that—
and he knew that he had coaxed her unschooled body
to an ecstasy that had shocked her with its intensity.
Knew that her ardent, bemused gaze in the sweet, exhausted aftermath of his lovemaking betokened just
what effect he'd had on her.

And if he wanted proof of that today—well, here

it was. She was gazing at him now with a look on her face that spread warmth through his whole being.

He brushed her lips with his again. Felt arousal—drowsy, dormant, but still present—start to stir. He deepened his kiss, using slow, sensuous, feather-light touches to stir within her an answering response. He would need to be gentle—very careful indeed—and take account of the dramatic changes to her body after their first union.

He felt her fingertips steal over his body, exploring…daring…fuelling his arousal with every tentative touch and glide…

With a deep, abiding satisfaction he started to make love to her again.

It was several days before they went to Athens. Days in which Tia knew she had, without the slightest doubt, been transported to a fantasy land.

How could she be anywhere else? She had been transported there by the most gorgeous, the most wonderful, the most shiveringly fabulous man she could ever have imagined! A man who had cast a glittering net of enchantment over her life.

That first morning, after he had made love to her again—and how was it possible for her body to feel what it did? She'd never known, never guessed that it was so—they'd breakfasted out on the little terrace, with the morning sun illuming them.

Then he'd whisked her off to one of the most famous luxury department stores in the world, from which she'd emerged, several hours later, with countless carrier bags of designer clothes and a new hairstyle—barely shorter, but so cunningly cut it had felt feather-light on her head, floating over her shoulders. Her make-up had been applied by an expert, and Anatole had smiled in triumphant satisfaction when he saw her.

I knew she could look fantastic with the right clothes and styling!

His eyes had worked over her openly, and he'd seen the flush of pleasure in her face. The glow in her eyes. Felt the warmth of it.

I've done the right thing—absolutely the right thing.

The certainty of that had streamed through him. This breathtakingly lovely creature that he'd scooped off the road and taken into his life was exactly right for him.

And so it had proved.

Taking Tia to Athens would only be the first of it.

He'd sorted out a passport for her—or rather, his office had—and they were now flying out...first class obviously.

For the entire flight she sat beside him in a state of stupefied bliss, sipping at her glass of champagne and gazing out through the porthole with a look of enchanted disbelief that this could really be happening to her.

In Athens, his chauffeured car was waiting to take him to his apartment—he did not use the Kyrgiakis mansion, far preferring his own palatial flat, with its stunning views of the Acropolis.

'Didn't I tell you that you should see the Parthenon one day?' he quizzed her smilingly, indicating the famous ruins visible from all around. 'It's not in the best of shape because the Ottomans used it as a gunpowder store, which exploded...' He grimaced. 'But it's being preserved as well as possible.'

'Ottomans?' Tia queried.

'They came out of what is now Turkey and conquered Greece in the fifteenth century—it took us four hundred years to be free.' Anatole explained.

Tia looked at him uncertainly. 'Was that Alexander the Great?' she asked tentatively, knowing that the famous character must come into Greek history somewhere.

Anatole's mouth twitched. 'Out by over two thousand years, I'm afraid. Alexander was before the Romans. Greece only became independent in modern times—during the nineteenth century.' He patted her hand. 'Don't worry about it. There's a huge amount of history in Greece. You'll get the hang of it eventually. I'll take you to the Parthenon while we're here.'

But in the end he didn't, because instead, business matters having been attended to, he decided to charter a yacht and take her off on an Aegean cruise.

His father had commandeered the Kyrgiakis yacht, but the one upon which he and Tia sailed off into the sunset was every bit as luxurious, and it reduced Tia to open-mouthed, saucer-eyed amazement.

'It's got a *helicopter!*' she breathed. 'And a swimming pool!'

'And another one indoors, in case it ever rains,' Anatole grinned. 'We'll go skinny-dipping in both!'

Colour flushed in her cheeks, and he found it endearing. He found everything about her endearing. Despite the fact that after a fortnight together she was *way* past being the virginal ingénue she'd been that first amazing night together, she was still delightfully shy.

But not so shy that she refused to go for a star-lit swim with him—the crew having been ordered to keep well below decks—nor declined to let him make love to her in the water, until she cried out with a smothered cry, her head falling back as he lifted her up onto his waiting body.

For ten days they meandered around the Aegean, calling in at little islands where he and Tia strolled along the waterfront, lunching in harbourside restaurants, or drove inland to picnic beneath olive groves, with the endless hum of the cicadas all about them.

Simple pleasures…and Anatole wondered when he had last done anything so peaceful with any female. Certainly not with any female who was as boundlessly appreciative as Tia was.

She adored everything they did together. Was thrilled by everything—whether it was taking the yacht's sailing dinghy to skim over the azure water to a tiny cove on a half-deserted island, where they lunched on fresh bread and olives and ripest peaches and then made love on the sand, washing off in the waves thereafter, or whether, like today, it was drinking a glass of Kir Royale and watching the sun set over a harbour bar, before returning to the yacht, moored out in the bay, for a five-course gourmet meal served on the upper deck by the soft-footed, incredibly attentive staff aboard, while music played from unseen speakers all around, the yacht moved on the slow swell of the sea and the moon rose out of the iridescent waters.

Tia gazed at Anatole across the damask tablecloth, over the candlelight between them.

'This is the most wonderful holiday I could ever have imagined!' she breathed.

Adoration was obvious in her eyes—for how could it not be? How could she not reveal all that she felt for this wonderful, incredible man who had brought her here? Emotion swelled within her like a billowing wave, almost overpowering her.

Anatole's dark eyes lingered on her lovely face. A warm, honeyed tan had turned her skin to gold, and her hair was even paler now from the sun's rays. He felt desire cream within him. How good she was for him, and how good he felt about her...about having her in his life.

'Tell me,' he said, 'have you ever been to Paris?'

Tia shook her head.

Anatole's smile deepened. 'Well, I have to go there on business. You'll love it!'

It felt good to know that he would be the first man to show her the City of Light. Just as it had felt good to take her on this cruise, to see her enjoy the luxury of his lifestyle. Good to see her eyes widen, her intake of breath—good to bestow his largesse upon her, for she was so appreciative of it.

King Cophetua, indeed.

But he liked the feeling. Liked it a lot. For her sake, obviously, he was finding pleasure in bestowing upon her the luxury and treats that had never come her way in her deprived life. But not just for her sake—he was honest enough to admit that. For himself too. It was very good to feel her ardent, adoring gaze upon him. It made him feel—warm.

Loved.

His mind sheered away from the word, as if hitting a rock in a stream. His expression changed as he negated what he'd just heard in his mind.

I don't want her to love me.

Of course he didn't! Love would be a completely unnecessary complication. They were having an affair, just as he'd had with all the women who had been in his life...in his bed. It would run its course and at some point they would part.

Until then—well, Tia, so unlike any other woman he'd known, was just what he wanted.

His only source of disquiet was that she remained so clearly uncomfortable whenever they were in company, wherever they travelled. He didn't want her feeling out of her depth in the inevitably cosmopolitan, sophisticated and wealthy circles he moved in, and he did his best to make things easier for her, but she was always very quiet.

Thoughts flickered uneasily in his head. Had anyone ever thought to ask the Beggar Maid how she'd felt after King Cophetua had plucked her up into his royal and gilded life?

And yet when they were alone she visibly relaxed, coming out of her shell, talkative and at ease. Happy just to be with him and endlessly appreciative. Endlessly desirous of him.

He was in no hurry, he realised, to part with her.

Will I ever be? he thought. Then he put the question out of his head. Whenever that time came, it was not now, and until it did he would enjoy this affair—enjoy Tia—to the full.

Tia sat at the vanity unit in the palatial en suite bathroom, gazing at her reflection. She was wearing one of the oh-so-many beautiful dresses Anatole had bought for her over the past months of their relationship. His generosity troubled her, but she had accepted it because she knew she couldn't move in his gilded world in her own inexpensive clothes.

And besides, none of these outfits are really mine! I wouldn't dream of taking them with me when—

Her mind cut out. She didn't want to think about that time. She didn't want it spoiling this wonderful, blissful time with Anatole.

Anatole! His very name brought a flush to her cheeks, a glow to her eyes. How wonderful he was— how kind, how *good* to her! Her heart beat faster every time she thought of him. With every glance she threw at him or he at her, she felt emotion burn in her, coursing through her veins.

She felt her expression change, and even as it did so her gaze became more troubled still, her eyes shadowing.

Be careful! Oh, be careful! There is only one way this affair can end when it does end—like fairy gold turning to dust at dawn! And the end will be bad for you—so, so bad.

But it would be worse—and the shadow in her eyes deepened, a chill icing down her veins—much, much worse, if she let her heart fill with the one emotion that it would be madness to feel for Anatole.

I long for the one thing that would keep me in Anatole's life for ever...

Anatole's mood was tense. They were back in Athens, and the annual Kyrgiakis Corp board meeting was looming. It never put him in a good mood. His parents would pester him for more money—sniping at each other across the table—and only the calming presence of his Uncle Vasilis would be any balm.

Putting in long hours at the Kyrgiakis Corp headquarters, closeted with his finance director going through all the figures and reports before the meeting, meant he'd had little time to devote to Tia lately, but when he did spend time with her he could sense that something was troubling her.

He'd had no time to probe, however—he'd told himself he would get this damn board meeting out of the way and then take her on holiday somewhere. The prospect had cheered him. But not enough to lift the perpetually grim expression on his face as he'd prepared for the coming ordeal.

Now, today, over breakfast, he was running through his head all that had to be in readiness for the meeting that morning,

As well as the official business his family would expect a lavish celebratory lunch, to be held at one of the best hotels in Athens where his father liked to stay. His mother, predictably, never stayed there, but at a rival hotel. They ran up huge bills at both, for they both put their stays on the business account—much to Anatole's irritation.

But his parents had always been a law unto themselves, and since he wanted as little to do with them as possible he tolerated their extravagance, and that of their current respective spouses, with gritted teeth. The only person he actually wanted to see was Vasilis, who'd been preoccupied in Turkey for some time now, helping one of the museums there in salvaging ancient artefacts from the ravages of war in the Middle East.

He'd invited Vasilis to lunch the day after the board

meeting, knowing that even though his scholarly uncle would be far too academic for Tia his kindly personality would not be intimidating to her.

He reached for his orange juice and paused. Tia was looking at him, her fingers twisting nervously in the handle of her coffee cup, with an expression on her face he'd never seen before in the many weeks they'd spent together.

'What is it?' he asked.

She didn't answer. Only swallowed. Paled. Her fingers twisted again.

'Tia?' he prompted.

Was there an edge in his voice? He didn't mean there to be, but he had to get on—time was at an absolute premium today, and he needed to eat breakfast and be gone. But maybe his tone *had* been a bit off, impatient, though he hadn't intended it to be, because she went even whiter. Bit her lip.

'Tell me,' he instructed, his eyes levelling on her.

Whatever was troubling her, he would deal with it later. For now he'd just offer some reassuring words— it was all he had time for. He set down his orange juice and waited expectantly. An anguished look filled her eyes and he saw her swallow again, clearly reluctant to speak.

When she did, he knew why. Knew with a cold, icy pool in his stomach.

Her voice was faint, almost a stammer.

'I... I think I may be pregnant...'

CHAPTER FOUR

CHRISTINE CLIMBED OUT of the car. Her legs were shaking. How she'd get indoors she did not know. Mrs Hughes, the housekeeper, was there already, having left the church before the committal, and she welcomed her in with a low, sad voice.

'A beautiful service, Mrs K,' she said kindly.

Christine swallowed. 'Yes, it was. The vicar was very good about allowing him a C of E interment considering he was Greek Orthodox.' She tried to make her voice sound normal and failed.

Mrs Hughes nodded sympathetically. 'Well, I'm sure the Good Lord will be welcoming Mr K, whichever door he's come into heaven through—such a lovely gentleman as he was, your poor husband.'

'Thank you.'

Christine felt her throat tighten, tears threaten. She went into her sitting room, throat aching.

The pale yellow and green trellis-pattern wallpaper was in a style she now knew was *chinoiserie*, just as she now knew the dates of all the antique furniture in the house, who the artists were of the Old Masters that hung on the walls, and the age and subject of the artefacts that Vasilis had so carefully had transferred from Athens to adorn the place he had come to call home, with his new young wife.

This gracious Queen Anne house in the heart of the Sussex countryside. Far away from his old life and far away from the shocked and outraged members of his family. A serene, beautiful house in which to live, quietly and remotely. In which, finally, to die.

Her tears spilled over yet again, and she crossed to the French window, looking out over the lawn. The gardens were not extensive, but they were very private, edged with greenery. Memory shot through her head of how she'd been so enchanted by the green oasis of Anatole's London roof terrace when he'd switched the lights on, turning it into a fairyland.

She sheared her mind away. What use to think… to remember? Fairyland had turned to fairy dust, and had been blown away in the chill, icy wind of reality. The reality that Anatole had spelt out to her.

'I have no intention of marrying you, Tia. Did you do this to try and get me to marry you?'

A shuddering breath shook her and she forced her shoulders back, forced herself to return to the present. She had not invited anyone back after the funeral—she couldn't face it. All she wanted was solitude.

Yet into her head was forced the image of the grim-faced, dark-suited man standing there, watching her at her husband's grave. Fear bit at her.

Surely he won't come here? Why would he? He's come to see his uncle buried, that's all. He won't sully his shoes by crossing this threshold—not while I'm still here.

But even as she turned from the window there came a knock on the door, and it opened to the housekeeper.

'I'm so sorry to disturb you, Mrs K, but you have a visitor. He says he's Mr K's nephew. I've shown him into the drawing room.'

Ice snaked down Christine's back. For a moment she could not move. Then, with an effort, she nodded.

'Thank you, Mrs Hughes,' she said.

Summoning all her strength, and all her courage, she went to confront the man who had destroyed all her naive and foolish hopes and dreams.

Anatole stood in front of the fireplace, looking around him with a closed, tight expression on his face, taking in the *objets d'art* and his uncle's beloved classical statuary, the Old Masters hanging on the panelled walls.

His mouth twisted. *She's done very well for herself, this woman I picked up from the street—*

Anger stabbed in him. Anger and so much more.

But anger was quite enough. She would be inheriting all Vasilis's share of the Kyrgiakis fortune—a handsome sum indeed. Not bad for a woman who'd once had to take any job she could, however menial and poorly paid, provided it came with accommodation.

Well, this job had certainly come with accommodation!

The twist of his mouth grew harsher. He had found a naïve waif and created a gold-digger…

I gave her a taste for all this. I turned her into this.

Sourness filled his mouth.

There were footsteps beyond the double doors and then they opened. His eyes snapped towards them as she stood there. He felt the blade of a knife stab into him as he looked at her. She was still in the black, tailored couture suit. Her hair was pulled back off her face into a tight chignon—no sign of the soft waves that had once played around her shoulders.

Her face was white. Stark. Still marked by tears shed at the graveside.

Memory flashed into his head of how she'd stood trembling beside the bonnet of his car as she broke down into incoherent sobs when he yelled at her for her stupidity in walking right in front of his car. How appalled he'd been at her reaction…how he'd wanted to stop those tears.

The blade twisted in him…

'What are you doing here?'

Her question was terse, tight-lipped, and she did not advance into the room, only closed the double doors behind her. There was something different about her voice, and it took Anatole a moment to realise that it was not just her blank, hostile tone, but her accent. Her voice was as crisp, as crystalline, as if she had been born to all this.

Her appearance echoed that impression. The severity of the suit, her hairstyle, and the poise with which she held herself, all contributed.

'My uncle is dead. Why else do you think I'm here?' His voice was as terse as hers. It was necessary to be so—it was vital.

Something seemed to pass across her eyes. 'Do you want to see his will? Is that it?'

There was defiance in her voice now—he could hear it.

A cynical cast lit his dark eyes. 'What for? He'll

have left you everything, after all.' He paused—a deadly pause. 'Isn't that why you married him?'

It was a rhetorical question, one he already knew the answer to.

She whitened, but did not flinch. 'He left some specific items for you. I'm going to have them couriered to you as soon as I've been granted probate.'

She paused, he could see it, as if gathering strength. Then she spoke again, her chin lifting, defiance in her voice—in her very stance.

'Anatole, why have you come here? What for? I'm sorry if you wanted the funeral to be in Athens. Vasilis specifically did not want that. He wanted to be buried here. He was friends with the vicar—they shared a common love of Aeschylus. The vicar read Greats at Oxford, and he and Vasilis would cap quotations with each other. They liked Pindar too—'

She broke off. Was she *mad*, rabbiting on about Ancient Greek playwrights and poets? What did Anatole care?

He was looking at her strangely, as if what she had said surprised him. She wasn't sure why. Surely he would not be surprised to find that his erudite uncle had enjoyed discussing classical Greek literature with a fellow scholar, even one so far away from Greece?

'The vicar is quite a Philhellene…' she said, her voice trailing off.

She took another breath. Got back to the subject in hand. Tension was hauling at her muscles, as if wires were suspending her.

'Please don't think of…of… I don't know…disinterring his coffin to take it back to Greece. He would not wish for that.'

Anatole gave a quick shake of his head, as if the thought had not occurred to him as he'd stood there, watching the farce playing out in the churchyard—Tia grieving beside the grave of the man she'd inveigled into committing the most outrageous act of folly—marrying her, a woman thirty years his junior.

'So what *are* you doing here?'

Her question came again, and he brought his mind back to it. What was he doing here? To put it into words was impossible. It had been an instinct—overpowering—an automatic decision not even consciously made. To... To what?

'I'm here to pay my respects,' he heard his own voice answer.

He saw her expression change, as if he'd just said something quite unbelievable.

'Well, not to *me*!' There was derision in her voice—but it was not targeted at him, he realised. He frowned, focussing on her face.

He felt his muscles clench. *Thee mou*, how beautiful she was! The natural loveliness that had so enchanted him, captivated him, that had inspired him so impulsively to take her into his life, had matured into true beauty. Beauty that had a haunting quality. A sorrow—

Does she feel sorrow at my uncle's death? Can she really feel that?

No, surely there could be only relief that she was now free of a man thirty years her senior—free to enjoy all the money he had left her. Yet again that spike drove into him. He hated what she had become. What he himself had made her.

'Anatole, I know perfectly well what you think of

me, so don't prate hypocrisies to me! Tell me why you're here.' And now he saw her shoulders stiffen, her chin rise defiantly. 'If it's merely to heap abuse on my head for having dared to do what I did, then I will simply send you packing. I'm not answerable to you and nor—' the tenor of her voice changed now, and there was a viciousness in it that was like the edge of a blade '—are you answerable to me, either. As you have already had occasion to point out!'

She took another sharp intake of breath.

'Our lives are separate—you made sure of that. And I... I accepted it. You gave me no choice. I had no claim on you—and you most certainly have no claim on me now, nor *any* say in my decisions. Or those your uncle made either. He married me of his own free will—and if you don't like that...well, get over it!'

If she'd sprouted snakes for hair, like Medusa, Anatole could not have been more shocked by her. Was *this* the Tia he remembered? This aggressive harpy? Lashing out at him, her eyes hard and angry?

Tia saw the shock in his face and could have laughed savagely—but laughing was far beyond her on this most gruelling of days. She could feel her heart-rate going insane and knew that she was in shock, as well as still feeling the emotional battering of losing Vasilis—however long it had been expected—and burying him that very day.

To have in front of her now the one man in the entire world she had dreaded seeing again was unbearable. It was unbearable to look at the man who had once been so dear to her.

She lifted a hand, as if to ward him off. 'Anatole, I don't know why you've come here, and I don't care—

we've nothing left to say to each other. Nothing!' She shut her eyes, then opened them again with a heavy breath. 'I'm sure you grieve for your uncle... I know you were fond of him and he of you. He did not seek this breach with you—'

She felt her throat closing again and could not continue. Wanted him only to go.

'What will you do with this place?'

Anatole's voice cut across her aching thoughts.

'I suppose you'll sell up and take yourself off to revel in your ill-gotten inheritance?'

She swallowed. How could it hurt that Anatole spoke to her in such a way? She knew what he thought of her marriage to Vasilis.

'I've no intention of selling up,' she replied coldly, taking protection behind her tone. 'This is my home, with many good memories.'

Something changed in his eyes. 'You'll need to live *respectably* here...' there was warning in his voice '...in this country house idyll in an English village.'

'I shall endeavour to do so.' Christine did not bother to keep the sarcasm out of her voice. Why should she? Anatole was making assumptions about her...as he had done before.

A stab went through her, painful and hurtful, but she ignored it.

Again something flashed in his eyes. 'You're a young woman still, Tia—and now that you have all my uncle's wealth to flaunt you can take your pick of men.' His voice twisted. 'And this time around they won't need to be thirty years older than you. You can choose someone young and handsome, even if they're penniless!'

His tone grew harsher still.

'I'd prefer it if you took yourself off to some flash resort where you can party all night and keep your married name out of the tabloid rags!'

Christine felt her expression harden. Was there any limit to how he was going to insult her? 'I'm in mourning, Anatole. I'm not likely to go off and party with hand-picked gigolos.'

She took another heaving breath, turning around to open the double doors.

'Please leave now, Anatole. We've nothing to say to each other. *Nothing.*'

Pointedly, she waited for him to walk into the wide, parquet-floored hall. There was no sign of Mrs Hughes, and Christine was glad. How much the housekeeper—or anyone else—knew about the Kyrgiakis clan, she didn't know and didn't want to think about. Providing everything was kept civil on the surface, that was all that mattered.

Anatole was simply her late husband's nephew, calling to pay his respects on his uncle's death. No reason for Mrs Hughes to think anything else.

With his long stride Anatole walked past her, and Christine caught the faint scent of his aftershave. Familiar—so very familiar.

Memory rushed through her and she felt her body sway with emotion. For a second it was so overwhelmingly powerful she wanted to catch his hand, throw herself into his arms, and sob. To feel his arms go about her, feel him hold her, cradle her, feel his strong chest support her, feel his closeness, his protection. Sob out her grief for his uncle—her grief for so much more.

But Anatole was gone from her. Separated from her as by a thousand miles, by ten thousand. Separated from her by what she had done—what he had *thought* she had done. There was nothing left to bring them together again—not now. Not ever.

This is the last time I shall set eyes on him. It has to be—because I could not bear to see him again.

There was a tearing pain inside her as these words framed in her head—a pain for all that had been, that had not been, that could never be...

He didn't look at her as he strode past her, as he headed for the large front door. His face was set, closed. She had seen it like that before, that last terrible day in Athens, and she had never wanted to see him look like that again. Like stone, crushing her pathetic hopes.

A silent cry came from her heart.

And then, from the top of the staircase that swept up from the back of the wide hallway to the upper storey of the house, came another cry. Audible this time.

'Mumma!'

Anatole froze. Not believing what he had heard. Froze with his hand on the handle of the door that would take him from the house, his heart infused with blackness.

Slowly he turned. Saw, as if in slow motion, a middle-aged woman in a nanny's uniform descending the stairs, holding by the hand a young child to stop him rushing down too fast. Saw them reach the foot of the staircase and the tiny figure tear across the hall to Tia. Saw her scoop him up, hug him, and set him down again gently.

'Hello, munchkin. Have you been good for Nanny?'

Tia's voice was warm, affectionate, and something about it caused a sliver of pain in Anatole's breast, penetrating his frozen shock.

'Yes!' the little boy cried. 'We've done painting. Come and see.'

'I will, darling, in a little while,' he heard her answer, with that same softness in her voice—a softness he remembered from long, long ago, that sent another sliver of pain through him.

The child's eyes went past her, becoming aware of someone standing by the front door.

'Hello,' he said in his piping voice.

His bright gaze looked right at Anatole. Clearly interested. Waiting for a response.

But Anatole could make none. Could only go on standing there, frozen, as knowledge forced itself into his head like a power hose being turned on.

Theos—she has a son.

He dragged his eyes from the child—the sable-haired, dark-eyed child—to the woman who was the boy's mother. Shock was in his eyes still. Shock, and more than shock. An emotion that seemed to well up out of a place so deep within him he did not know it was there. He could give it no name.

'I didn't know—' His voice broke off.

Did her hand tighten on the child's? He could see her face take on an expression of reserve, completely at odds with the warmth of a moment again when she'd been hugging her child.

'Why should you?' she returned coolly. Her chin lifted slightly. 'This is Nicky.' Her eyes dropped to her son. 'Nicky, this is your—'

She stopped. For a second it seemed to Anatole that a kind of paralysis had come over her face.

It was he who filled the gap. Working out just what his relationship was to the little boy. 'Your cousin,' he said.

Nicky cast him an even more interested look. 'Have you come to play with me?' he asked.

Immediately both his nanny and his mother intervened.

'Now, Nicky, not *everyone* who comes here comes to play with you,' his nanny said, her reproof very mild and given as if it were a routine reminder.

'Munchkin, no—your…your cousin is here because of poor Pappou—'

The moment she spoke Christine wished desperately that she hadn't. But she was in no state to think straight. It was taking every ounce of what little remaining strength she had just to remain where she was, to cope with this nightmare scenario playing out, helpless to stop it. Helpless to do anything but hang on in there until finally—dear God, *finally*—the front door closed behind Anatole and she could collapse.

'Pappou?'

The single word from Anatole was like a bullet. A bullet right through her. She stared, aghast at what she'd said.

Grandfather.

She could only stare blindly at Anatole. She had to explain, to make sense of what she'd said—what she'd called Vasilis.

But she was spared the ordeal. At her words Nicky's little face had crumpled, and she realised with a knife in her heart that she had made an even worse mistake than saying what she had in front of Anatole.

'Where is he? I want him—I *want* him! I want Pappou!'

She dropped to her knees beside him, hugging him as he sobbed, giving him what comfort she could, reminding him of how Pappou had been so ill, and was now in heaven, where he was well again, where they would see him again one day.

Then, suddenly there was someone else hunkering down beside her and Nicky. Someone resting his hand on Nicky's heaving shoulder.

Anatole spoke, his voice a mix of gentleness and kindness, completely different from any tone she'd heard from him so far in this nightmare encounter. 'Did you say that you've been doing some painting with Nanny?'

Christine felt Nicky turn in her arms, look at the man kneeling down so close. She saw her son nod, his face still crumpled with tears.

'Well,' said Anatole, in the same tone of voice but now with a note of encouragement in it, 'why don't you paint a picture especially for…for Pappou?'

He said the word hesitantly, but said it all the same. His tone of voice changed again, and now there was something new in it.

'When I was little, I can remember I painted a picture for…for Pappou. I painted a train. It was a bright red train. With blue wheels. You could paint one too, if you like, and then he would have one from both of us. How would that be?'

Christine saw her son gaze at Anatole. Her throat

felt very tight. As tight as if wire had been wrapped around it—barbed wire that drew blood.

'Can my train be blue?' Nicky asked.

Anatole nodded. 'Of course it can. It can be blue with red wheels.'

Nicky's face lit up, his tears gone now. He looked across to his nanny, standing there, ready to intervene if that were needed. Now it was.

'What a good idea!' she said enthusiastically. 'Shall we go and do it now?'

She held out her hand and Nicky disengaged himself from his mother, trotting up to his nanny and taking her hand. He turned back to Christine. 'Nanny and me are going to paint a picture for Pappou,' he informed her.

Christine gave a watery smile. 'That's a lovely idea, darling,' she said.

'Will you show it to me when you've done it?' It was Anatole who'd spoken, rising to his feet, looking across at the little boy.

Nicky nodded, then tugged on his nanny's hand, and the two of them made their journey back up the stairs, with Nicky talking away animatedly.

Christine watched them go. Her heart was hammering in her chest, so loudly she was sure it must be audible. A feeling of faintness swept over her as she stood up.

Did she sway? She didn't know—knew only that a hand had seized her upper arm, was steadying her. A hand that was like a vice.

Had Anatole done that only to stop her fainting? Or for another reason?

She jerked herself free, stepped back sharply. To have him so close—so close to Nicky...

He spoke, his voice low, so as not to be within earshot of the nanny, but his tone was vehement.

'I had no idea—*none!*'

Christine trembled, but her voice was cool. 'Like I said, why should you? If Vasilis chose not to tell you, *I* was hardly likely to!'

Anatole's dark eyes burned into hers. She felt faintness drumming at her again. Such dark eyes...

So like Nicky.

No—she must not think that. Vasilis's eyes had been dark as well, typically Greek. And brown was genetically dominant over her own blue eyes. Of course Nicky would have the dark eyes of his father's family.

'Why does the boy call my uncle *pappou*?' The demand was terse—requiring an answer.

She took a careful breath. 'Vasilis thought it... wiser,' she said. Her mouth snapped closed. She did not want to talk about it, discuss it, have it questioned or challenged.

But Anatole was not to be silenced. 'Why?' he said bluntly.

His eyes seemed to be burning into hers. She rubbed a hand over her forehead. A great weariness was descending on her after the strain of the last grim months—Vasilis's final illness, the awfulness of the last fortnight since he'd died, and now, the day of her husband's burial, the nightmare eruption into her life of the man who had caused her marriage to Vasilis.

'Vasilis knew his heart was weak. That it would give out while Nicky was still young. So he said...' Her voice wavered and she took another difficult breath, not wanting to look at Anatole but knowing she *must* say what she had to. 'He said it would be… kinder for Nicky to grow up calling him his grand-father.'

She had to fight to keep her lips from trembling, her eyes from filling with tears. Her hands clenched each other, nails digging into her palms.

'He said Nicky would miss him less when the time came, feel less deprived than if he'd thought of him as his father.'

Anatole was silent but his thoughts were hectic, heaving. And as troubled as a stormy night. Emotion writhed within him. Memory slashed across his synapses. He could hear Tia's voice—his own.

'I have no intention of being a father—so do not even think of forcing my hand!'

Christine looked at him, her expression veiled. See-ing his—guessing what he was remembering.

'Given what has happened,' she said quietly, 'Vasilis made the right decision. Nicky will have only dim memories of him as he grows, but they will be very fond ones and I will always honour Vasilis's memory to him.'

She swallowed, then said what she must.

'Thank you for suggesting he paint Vasilis a pic-ture. It was a very good idea—it diverted him per-fectly.'

'I can remember—just—painting the picture for my uncle that I told Nicky about. He'd come to visit and I was excited. He always brought me a present and paid attention to me. Spent time with me. Later I re-alised he'd come to talk to my father, to tell him that, for my sake, my father should…mend his ways.' His mouth twisted. 'He had a wasted journey. My father was incapable of mending his ways.'

He frowned, as if he had said too much. He took a ragged breath, shook his head as if to clear it of memories that had no purpose any more.

Then he let his eyes rest on Tia.

'We need to talk,' he said.

CHAPTER FIVE

CHRISTINE SAT ON the chintz-covered sofa, tension racking her still as Mrs Hughes set out a tray of coffee on the ormolu table at her side. Her throat was parched and she was desperate for a shot of caffeine—anything to restore her drained energy levels.

In her head, memory cut like a knife.

'I could murder a cup of coffee.'

Anatole had said that the very first afternoon he'd picked her up off the street where she'd fallen in front of his car and brought her back to his flat. Was he remembering it too? She didn't know. His expression was closed.

As her eyes flickered over him she felt emotion churn in her stomach. His physical impact on her was overpowering. As immediate and overwhelming as it had been the very first time she'd set eyes on him. The five years since she had last set eyes on him vanished.

Panic beat in her again.

I've got to make him go away. I've got to—

'You realise that this changes everything—the fact that Vasilis has a son?'

She started, staring at Anatole. 'Why?' she said blankly.

He lifted an impatient hand, a coffee cup in it, before drinking. 'Don't be obtuse,' he said. 'That is, don't be stupid—'

'I know what obtuse means!' she heard herself snap at him.

He paused, rested his eyes on her. He said nothing, but she could see that her sharp tone had taken him by surprise. He wasn't used to her talking to him like that. Wasn't used to hostility from her.

'It changes nothing that he has a son.' Her voice trembled on the final word. Had Anatole noticed the tremor? She hoped not.

'Of course it does!' he replied.

He finished his coffee, roughly set the cup back on the tray. He was on the sofa opposite her, but he was still too close. His eyes flickered over her for a moment, but his expression was still veiled.

'I will not have Nicky punished for what you did.' He spoke quietly, but there was an intensity in his voice that was like a chill down her spine, 'I will not have him exiled from his family just because of you. He needs his family.'

Her coffee cup rattled on its saucer as her hand trembled. 'He *has* a family—*I* am his family!'

Anatole's hand slashed down. 'So am I! And he cannot be raised estranged from his kin.' He took a heavy breath. 'Whatever you have done, Tia, the boy must not pay for it. I want—'

Something snapped inside her. 'What *you* want, Anatole, is irrelevant! *I* am Nicky's mother. I have sole charge of him, sole guardianship. *I*—not you, and not anyone else in the entire world—get to say any single thing about how he grows up, and in whose company, or any other detail of his life. *Do you understand me?*'

She saw his face whiten around his mouth. Again, it was as if she had sprouted snakes for hair.

Stiffly, he answered her. 'I understand that you have been under considerable strain. That whatever your...your feelings you have had to cope with Vasilis's final illness and his death. His funeral today. You are clearly under stress.'

He got to his feet.

How tall he seemed, towering over her as she sat, her legs too weak, suddenly, to support her in standing up to face him.

He looked at her gravely, his face still shuttered.

'It has been a difficult day,' he said, his voice tight. 'I will take my leave now...let you recover. But...'

He paused, then resumed, never taking from her his dark, heavy gaze that pressed like weights on raw flesh.

'But this cannot be the end of the matter. You *must* understand that, Tia. You must accept it.'

She pushed herself to her feet. 'And *you*, Anatole, must accept that you have nothing to do with my child. *My* child.'

The emphasis was clear. Bitter. Darkness flashed in her eyes, and she lifted her chin defiantly, said the words burning in her like brands.

'I don't want you coming here again. You've made your opinion of me very, very clear. I don't want you coming near my son—*my* son! He has quite enough to bear, in losing Vasilis, without having your hatred of me to cope with. I won't have you poisoning his ears with what you think of me.'

She took a sharp breath, her eyes like gimlets, spearing him.

'Stay away, Anatole. Just *stay away*!'

She marched to the drawing room doors, yanking them open. Her heart was thumping in her breast, her chest heaving. She had to get him out of her house—right now.

Wordlessly, Anatole strode past her. This time—*dear God*—this time she would get him out of the house.

Only at the front door did he turn. Pause, then speak. 'Tia—'

'That is no longer my name.' Christine's voice was stark, biting across him, her face expressionless. 'I stopped being Tia a long time ago. Vasilis always called me Christine, my given name, not any diminutive. I am Christine. That's who I am—who I always will be.'

There was a choke in her voice as grief threatened her. But grief was not her greatest threat. Her greatest threat was the man it always had been.

Her nails pressed into her palms and she welcomed the pain. She turned away, leaving him to let himself out, rapid footsteps impelling her towards the door of her sitting room. She gained it, shut the door behind her, leaning against it, feeling faintness threatening. Her eyes were stark and staring. That barbed wire garrotting her throat.

I will never be Tia again. I can never be Tia again.

The barbed wire pressed tighter yet. Now it was drawing blood.

Anatole drove up the motorway, back towards London. He was pushing the speed limit and did not care. He needed to put as much distance as he could between himself and Tia.

Christine.

That was what she called herself now, she'd said. What his uncle had called her. His eyes shifted. He did not want to think about his uncle calling Tia… Christine…anything at all. Having anything to do with her.

Having a child with her.

His mind sheared away. No, he could not think about that—about the creation of a child between Tia and his uncle—his erudite bachelor uncle who'd never had a romance in his life.

And still never had, either—whatever lures Tia had cast over him.

His expression changed. No, that was the wrong way to look at it—they could not have been lures. Vasilis would have been immune to anything so crude.

She would just have come across as helpless and vulnerable. Cast aside by me—

His mind shifted away again. He still did not want to think about it. Didn't want to remember that day five long years ago.

Yet memory came, all the same…

'I… I think I may be pregnant.'

The words fell into the space between them.

Anatole could feel himself freezing, hear himself responding.

'So are you or aren't you?'

That was what he said. A simple question.

He saw, as if from a long way away, her face blanch.

'I'm not sure,' she whispered, expression strained. 'My period is late—'

'How late?' Again, a simple question.

'I… I think it's about a week late. I… I'm not sure. It may be longer.'

Anatole found himself trying to calculate in his head when she'd last been…indisposed. Could not quite place it. But that wasn't relevant. Only one thing mattered now.

His voice seemed to come from a long way away. A long way from where she was sitting, gazing at him, her expression like nothing he had ever seen before. Like nothing he wanted to see.

'You'd better do a test.' The words came out clipped, completely unemotional. 'With luck it's a false alarm.'

Without luck—

His mind sheared away. He would not think about the alternative. But even as he steeled himself he narrowed his eyes, resting them on her face. There was a stricken look on it, but something more, too.

She's hiding something.

Every instinct told him that. She was concealing something, pushing it back inside her, so that he could not tell what it was. But he knew—oh, he knew.

I haven't given her the right answer—the answer she wanted to hear. I've caught her out by not giving her that answer, and she doesn't know how to react now.

He knew what she'd wanted his reaction to be. It was obvious. He was supposed to have reacted very differently from the way he had.

I was supposed to look amazed—thrilled. I was supposed to sweep her up into my arms. Tell her she was the most treasured thing in the universe to me, carrying my oh-so-precious child! I was supposed

*to tell her that I was thrilled beyond everything—
that she'd given me the best gift I could ever have
dreamt of!*

And then, of course, he was supposed to have gone
down on one knee, taken her hand in his, and asked
her to marry him.

Because that was what they *all* wanted, didn't they?
All the women who passed through his life. They
wanted him to marry them.

And he was so tired of it—so bored, so exasperated.

All of them wanted to be Mrs Kyrgiakis. As if there
weren't three of them already—his father's current
wife and his two exes. Even his mother had coupled
her new husband's name to Kyrgiakis, to ensure so
she got kudos from the family connection as well as
her hand in the Kyrgiakis coffers.

So, no, with quite enough Mrs Kyrgiakises in the
world, he did not want another one.

Not another one who had only become one because
she was pregnant—the way his mother had become
Mrs Kyrgiakis the Second. Giving her the perfect opportunity to dump her unwanted first husband and
snap up a second. Not that she'd wanted his father for
long, or he her. They'd both got bored and taken lovers, and then another spouse each. Creating yet another Mrs Kyrgiakis.

And so the circus had gone on.

I will not perpetuate it.

Not willingly. *Never* willingly—

His eyes rested on Tia, his expression veiled. She
was looking pale and nervous. He reached out a hand
as if to touch her cheek, reassure her. Then he pulled
back. What reassurance could he give her? He didn't

want to marry her. That would hardly reassure her, would it?

'Did you do it deliberately? Take a chance that you might get pregnant?'

The words were out of his mouth before he could stop them. He heard her gasp, saw her face blanch again. As if he had slapped her.

But he could not unsay them—un-ask the question he'd pushed at her.

'Well?' he persisted.

His eyes were still resting on her, no expression in them, because he did not want to let his feelings show. He needed to keep them banked down, suppressed.

He saw her swallow, shake her head.

'Well, that's something,' he breathed. 'So, how did it happen? How is it even a possibility?'

She'd been on the Pill for months now. Ever since he'd made the decision to keep her in his life. So what had gone wrong?

He saw her drop her eyes, her face convulse. 'It was when we went to San Francisco. The changing time zones muddled me.'

He gave a heavy sigh. He should have checked— made sure she hadn't got 'muddled'.

'Well, hopefully it hasn't screwed things up completely.'

Her expression changed. Anxiety visible. But there was another emotion too. One he could not name. Did not want to.

'Would it?' Her voice was thin, as if stretched too far. Her eyes were searching his. '*Would* it screw things up completely?'

He turned away. Reached for his briefcase. It was

going to be a long, draining day—getting through the annual board meeting, seeing his parents again, watching them pointedly ignore each other, pointedly show demonstrations of affection to their current new spouses, glaring testimony to the shallow fickleness of their emotions, constantly imagining themselves in love, rushing into yet another reckless, ill-considered marriage.

No wonder he didn't want to marry—didn't want to be cornered into marrying by any woman prepared to do anything to get his ring on her finger. Including getting herself pregnant.

I didn't think Tia was like that. I thought what we had suited her, just like it suited me. I thought that she was fond of me, as I am of her—but there's nothing about love. Nothing about marriage. And, dear God, nothing about babies!

But it looked as if he'd been wrong—

He didn't answer her. Couldn't answer her. Instead he simply glanced at his watch—he was running late already.

He looked back at her as he headed for the door, not meeting her eyes. 'I'll have a pregnancy testing kit delivered,' he said—and was gone.

There was a tight wire around his throat. He felt its pressure for the rest of the day. All through the gruelling board meeting—his parents behaving just as he'd known they would, constantly pressing for yet more profits to be distributed to them. And after the meeting was the even more gruelling ordeal of an endlessly long lunch that went on all afternoon.

'You seem distracted, Anatole. Is everything all right?'

This was his Uncle Vasilis, taking the opportunity to draw him aside after the formal meal had finally finished and everyone was milling about, lighting up cigars, drinking vintage port and brandy.

'Call me old-fashioned,' Vasilis said, 'but when a young man is distracted it is usually by a woman.'

He paused again, his eyes studying Anatole even though Anatole had immediately, instinctively, blanked his expression. But it did not silence his uncle.

'You know,' Vasilis continued, 'I would so like you to fall in love and marry—make a *happy* marriage! Yes, I know you are sceptical, and I can understand why—but do not judge the world by your parents. They constantly imagine themselves in love with yet another object of their desire. Making a mess of their lives, being careless of everyone else's. Including,' he added, his eyes not shifting from Anatole's face, 'yours.'

Anatole's mouth tightened. *Making a mess of their lives...* Was that what *he* was going to do too? Had he already done it? Was he simply waiting to find out whether it was so?

Does she have the results already? Does she know if she's messed up my life—and I hers?

But a darker question was already lurking beneath those questions. Would being pregnant by him mess up Tia's life or achieve a dream for her? Attain her goal—her ambition.

Have I given her a taste for the life I lead, so that now she wants to keep it for herself, for ever?

Having a Kyrgiakis child would achieve that for her. A Kyrgiakis child would achieve a Kyrgiakis husband. Access to the Kyrgiakis coffers. To the lavish Kyrgiakis lifestyle.

'Anatole?'

His uncle's voice penetrated his circling thoughts, his turbid emotions. But he could not cope with an inquisition now, so he only gave a brief smile and asked his uncle about his latest philanthropic endeavour.

Vasilis responded easily enough, but Anatole was aware of concern in his uncle's eyes, a sense that he was being studied, worried over. He blanked it, just as he was blanking the question that had been knifing in his head all day. Did Tia have her results, and—dear God—what were they?

He wanted to phone her, but dreaded it too. So much hung in the balance—his whole future depended on Tia's answer.

As everyone finally dispersed from the hotel—Vasilis departing with a smile and saying he was looking forward to accepting his nephew's lunch invitation the next day, an invitation Anatole now wished he'd never made—he found that he actually welcomed his father catching him by the arm and telling him, in a petulant undertone, that thanks to the booming profits Anatole had just announced his latest wife had suddenly decided to divorce him.

'You've made me too rich!' he accused his son illtemperedly. 'So now I need you to find a way to make sure she gets as little as possible.'

He dragged Anatole off to a bar, pouring into his son's ears a self-pitying moan about greedy ex-wives, and how hard done by he was by them all, while he proceeded to work his way through a bottle of whisky.

Eventually Anatole returned him to his hotel room

and left him. Finally heading back to his apartment, he felt his heart start to hammer. He could postpone finding out Tia's results no longer.

Yet when he reached his apartment, close to midnight, Tia was asleep. He did not disturb her. Could not. Of the pregnancy test kit there was no sign, and he had no wish to search for it in the bathroom, to see the result—to know what his future would be. Not now, not yet...

With that wire tightening around his throat, he stood gazing down at her. She looked so small in the huge king-sized bed. Emotions flitted across the surface of her mind. Emotions he had never had cause to feel before. Thoughts he had never had to think before.

Is she carrying my child? Does it grow within her body?

Those emotions flickered again, like currents of electricity, static that could not flow, meeting resistance somewhere in the nerve fibres of his brain.

Yet he could feel the impulse to let it flow, connect, let it overcome him—so that almost, almost he stripped off his clothes to lie own with her, take her into his arms, not to make love to her, but to hold her slender, petite body, to slide his hand across her abdomen where, right now, secret and safe, their baby might be taking hold of life. To hold them both, close and cherishing...

He stepped away. He must not let himself succumb. Must do what he was doing now—walking away, taking himself off to another bedroom, sleeping there the night, his dreams troubled and troubling.

He woke the next morning to see Tia standing in

the doorway, her body silhouetted in her nightgown by the morning sun.

'I'm not pregnant,' she said to him. 'I've just got my period.' There was no emotion in her voice. Nor in her face.

Then she turned and left.

Anatole lay motionless, his open eyes staring at the ceiling, where sunlight played around the light socket. It was very strange. Her announcement should have brought relief. Should have made everything well between them.

Yet it had ended everything.

CHAPTER SIX

CHRISTINE SAT AT the desk in Vasilis's study. She could feel the echo of him here still—here where he had spent so much of his time—and found comfort in it.

The weeks since his death had turned into months. Slow, painful, difficult months of getting used to a house empty of his quiet presence. It had been difficult for her, difficult for Nicky. Tears and tantrums had been frequent as the little boy had slowly, unwillingly come to terms with the loss of his beloved *pappou*.

Pappou—the word stabbed into Christine's head, and again she heard Anatole's shock. Her mind closed, automatically warding off the memory of that nightmare encounter with the man she had fled. Who had not wanted her as she had wanted him. Who thought of her as nothing more than a cheap adventuress...a gold-digger who had married his uncle for the wealth he could bestow upon her.

Pain hacked at her at the thought of how badly Anatole regarded her. How much he seemed to hate her now.

She had been right to send him packing. Anything else would have been unbearable! Unthinkable. Yet even as she felt that resolve she felt another emotion too. Powerful—painful. Nicky had done the painting of a train for his *pappou* and he wanted to know when his 'big cousin' was going to come and see it.

She had given evasive answers—he lived in Greece, Pappou's homeland, and he was very busy, working very hard.

After a while Nicky had stopped asking, but every now and then he would still say 'I *want* to see him again! Why can't I see him again? I painted the picture! I want to show it to him!' And then he'd become tearful and difficult.

Guilt stabbed at Christine. Her son was going through so much now. And he always would. He would be growing up without Vasilis in his life, without the man he thought of as his grandfather.

Growing up without a father—

Her mind sheared away. What use was it to think of that? *None.* Instead, she took a breath, focussing her attention on what she needed to do right now.

Probate had finally been completed—a lengthy task, given that Vasilis's estate was large, his will complex, and it had involved the setting up of both a family trust and a philanthropic foundation to carry on his work.

It was the latter that preoccupied her now. At the end of the week she was going to have to perform her first duty as Vasilis's widow—to represent him at the opening of an exhibition of Greek art and antiquities at a prestigious London museum. Though she had always accompanied him to the events he'd sponsored, this was the first time she would be alone. It was a daunting prospect, but she was resolved to perform to the best of her ability. She owed it to Vasilis to do so.

Now, in preparation, she bowed her head to read through the correspondence and the detailed notes from the curator, to make sure she knew what she must know in time for the event.

This is for Vasilis. For him who gave me so much!

It was a fraction of what she owed him—the man who had rescued her when her life had been at its lowest, most desolate ebb.

Anatole was in a business meeting, but his mind was not on the involved mesh of investments, profits and tax exposure that was its subject. Instead he was focussed mentally on the request he had received that morning from his uncle's lawyers in London. They wanted him to contact them. Probate, apparently, had now been completed.

His mouth thinned. So now he would find out just how rich Vasilis's young widow would be. Just how much she had profited from marrying his middle-aged uncle. Oh, she had done very well indeed out of convincing him to marry her. To rescue her from Anatole, the man who had lifted her—literally—off the street!

I thought she was so devoted to me. But all along it was just the lifestyle I gave her. She couldn't wait to ensure it for herself by getting Vasilis's wedding ring on her finger after I'd made it clear to her that any hope she might have had of letting herself get pregnant to get me to marry her was out of the question.

That old familiar stab came again. It was anger— of *course* it was anger! What else could it be? It was anger that he felt when he thought about Tia abandoning him to snap up his uncle. Only anger.

Restlessly, Anatole shifted in his seat, impatient for

the meeting to be done. Yet when he finally was free to get back to his office, to phone London, he knew he was reluctant to do so.

Did he really want to stir up in himself again those mixed emotions that his uncle's death had caused? That his rash visit to England on the day of the funeral had plunged him into? Shouldn't he just leave things be? He could not alter his uncle's will—if his widow had all Vasilis's money to splurge, so what? Why should he care?

Except that—

Except that it is not just about Tia, is it? Or about you. There's someone else to think about.

Vasilis's son. Nicky. The little boy he'd known nothing about—never guessed existed.

That scene burned in his head again—himself hunkering down to offer solace to the heartbroken child. Emotion thrust inside him, but a new one now—one that seemed to pierce more deeply than the thought that the woman he had once romanced, made love to, taken into his life, had abandoned him. It was a piercing that came from the sobs of a bereft child, that made him want to comfort him, console him.

He stared sightlessly across his office. Where did that emotion come from? *Never* had he thought about children—except negatively. Oh, not because he disliked them, but because they had nothing to do with him. Could never have anything to do with him. What he'd said to Tia, that grim day when she'd thought she was pregnant, was as true now as it had been then.

And yet—

What instinct had made him seek to comfort the

little boy? To divert him, bring a smile to his face, light up his eyes?

It's because he's Vasilis's son. Because he has no one else to look out for him now. Only a mother who married his father just to endow herself with a wealthy lifestyle she could never have aspired to otherwise.

His expression changed. Turned steely. He had told Tia that Nicky's existence changed everything but she had rejected what he'd said. Sent him from her house. Banned him from making any contact with Nicky. His eyes darkened. Well, that was not going to happen. *Someone* had to look out for Vasilis's child, and now that his widow had a free rein with her late husband's wealth she could do anything she wanted with it! What security would there be for Vasilis's son when his mother was an ambitious, luxury-loving gold-digger?

The phone on his desk sounded, indicating the call to London was ready for him. Grim-faced, he picked it up. Whatever he had to do, he would ensure that his vulnerable young cousin was not left to the mercy of his despised mother.

I'll fight her for justice for her son—for Vasilis's son.

Yet when he slowly hung up the phone, some ten minutes later, his expression was different. Very different. He called through to his secretary.

'Book me on the next flight to London.'

Christine sat back in the car that was taking her up to London for the evening. Her nerves were jittery, and not just because she would be representing Vasilis at the exhibition's opening. It was also because this would be the first time she'd been to London since he'd died—and London held memories that were of more than her husband.

She felt her mind shear away. No, she must not think—must not remember how she had met Anatole, how he had swept her into his life, how she had fallen head over heels for a man who had been to her eyes like a prince out of a fairytale!

But he hadn't been a prince after all. He'd been an ordinary person, however rich and gilded his existence, and he'd had no desire for her to be a permanent part of his life. No desire at all for a baby...a child.

It was Vasilis who'd wanted that. Had wanted the child who'd given him a joy that, as Christine sadly knew, he'd never thought to have.

The knowledge comforted her.

However much he gave me—immense though that was, and eternally grateful though I am—I know that I gave him Nicky to love...

Now she was all Nicky had.

Her nerves jangled again. She must not think of Anatole, must only be grateful that he'd accepted her dismissal. Had made no further attempt to get in touch. Make contact with Nicky.

Her mouth set. Eyes stark.

His knowing of Nicky's existence doesn't change anything. And I won't—I won't!—have anyone near Nicky who thinks so ill of me, poisoning my son's mind against me...

For the remainder of the journey she forced herself to focus only on the evening's event.

Later, when the moment came, she felt a sudden tightening of her throat as she was introduced as Mrs

Vasilis Kyrgiakis, then she took a measured breath and began her short, carefully written speech. She said how pleased her husband had been to support this important exhibition of Hellenistic art and artefacts, so expertly curated by the museum—giving a smiling nod to the director, Dr Lanchester—and then diverted a little on descriptions of some of the key exhibits, before concluding with a reassurance that despite Vasilis Kyrgiakis's untimely death his work was being entrusted to a foundation specifically set up for that purpose.

After handing over to Dr Lanchester she stepped away, and as the formal opening was completed started to mingle socially with the invited guests.

Everyone was in evening dress, and although, of course, her dress was black, her state of mourning did not prevent her from accepting a proffered glass of champagne. She sipped it delicately, listening to something the director's wife was saying, and smiling appropriately. She knew both the director and his wife, having dined with them together with Vasilis, before his final illness had taken its fatal grip on him.

She was about to make some remark or other when a voice behind her turned her to stone.

'Won't you introduce me?'

She whipped round, not believing her eyes. But it was impossible to deny who she was seeing.

Anatole.

Anatole in a black tuxedo, like all the other male guests, towering over her.

Shock made faintness drum in her head.

How on earth? What on earth?

He gave a swift, empty smile. 'I felt it my duty to represent the Kyrgiakis family tonight,' he informed her.

If it was meant as a barb, implying that *she* could not possibly do so, she did not let her reaction show. She gave a grave nod.

'I'm sure Vasilis would have appreciated your presence here,' she acknowledged quietly. 'He worked hard to ensure this exhibition would be possible. Many of the artefacts have been rescued from the turmoil in the Middle East, to find safety here, for the time being, until eventually they can be securely returned.'

She indicated with a graceful gesture towards some of the exhibits to which she was referring, but Anatole was not looking. His eyes were only on her. Taking her in. The woman standing there, in a black silk evening gown, with long sleeves and a high-cut neckline, was every inch in mourning, but she was not a woman Anatole recognised.

He'd arrived to see her take centre stage, and had not believed it could be Tia—*Christine*—Vasilis's widow. Poised, elegant, mature—and perfectly capable of addressing a room full of learned dignitaries and opening an exhibition of Hellenistic archaeology.

No, she was definitely not the socially nervous, timid Tia he remembered.

Nor was it the Tia he remembered who was turning now towards the museum's director.

'Dr Lanchester—may I introduce Vasilis's nephew, Anatole Kyrgiakis?'

If there was any tremor in her voice Anatole did not hear it. Her composure was perfect. Only the sudden masking in her eyes as she'd first seen him there had revealed otherwise. And that masking came again as the museum director smiled at Anatole.

'Will you be taking on your uncle's role?' he asked.

'Alas, I will be unable to become as directly involved as he was, but I hope to be one of the trustees of the foundation,' Anatole replied easily. 'Along with, I'm sure, my...' He hesitated slightly, turning to Christine. 'I'm not sure quite what our relationship is,' he said.

Was that another barb? She ignored it, as she had the first. 'I doubt it has a formal designation,' she remarked, with dogged composure. 'And, yes, I shall be one of the foundation's trustees.'

Her mouth tightened. *And no way on earth will I let you be one too!*

The very thought of having to attend trustees' meetings with Anatole there—she felt a cold chill through her. Then he was speaking again. He was smiling a courtesy smile, but she could see the dark glint in his eyes.

'I do hope, then, that you no longer believe Alexander the Great to be contemporary with the Greek War of Independence!' he said lightly.

Did he mean to wound her? If he did, then it only showed how bitter he was towards her.

Before, when she had been Tia—ignorant, uneducated Tia, who'd spent her schooldays nursing her mother—he'd never been anything other than sympathetic towards her in her lack of knowledge of all that he took for granted with his expensive private education.

But he'd meant to wound her now, and she would not let him do so.

So she only smiled in return, not looking at him but at the others. 'Before I married Vasilis,' she explained, 'I was completely ignorant of a great deal of history. But I *do* now know that in the fourth century BC Alexander was pre-dating the Battle of Navarino in 1827 by quite some time!'

Her expression was humorous. It had to be. How else could she deal with this?

'I think—at least, I *hope*!—that now, thanks to Vasilis's tuition, I can recognise the Hellenistic style, at least in obvious examples. Speaking of which…' she turned to the curator of the exhibition and bestowed an optimistic smile upon him '… I wonder if I might impose on you to guide me around the exhibits?'

'I'd be delighted!' he assured her, and to her profound relief she was able to move away.

Nevertheless, as she was conducted around she was burningly conscious of Anatole's presence in all the rooms.

She prayed that she would not have to talk to him again. Why had he turned up? Had he meant it, saying he wanted to be one of the foundation's trustees? What power would she have to prevent him? After all, he was a Kyrgiakis—how could she object?

But perhaps he only said it to get at me. Just like he made that reference to how ignorant I once was…

She felt a little sting inside her. Did he truly hate her so much? Her throat tightened. Of course he did! Hadn't he said it to her face, the day of Vasilis's funeral, calling her such vile names?

But you didn't want me, Anatole—and Vasilis did! So why berate me for accepting what he offered with such kindness, such generosity?

The answer was obvious, of course. Five long years of anger were driving him, and Anatole believed that she had manoeuvred Vasilis into marrying her so that she could enjoy the lavish Kyrgiakis lifestyle he provided. For no other reason.

A great sense of weariness washed over her. The strain of having to represent Vasilis tonight, the poignancy of the occasion and then the shock of Anatole intruding, the barbs he had directed at her—were all overpowering her.

Forcing herself to make some kind of appropriate response to the curator as he introduced each exhibit, she counted the minutes until she could decently call a halt. She had to get away—escape.

Finally, murmuring her excuses—readily accepted, given her mourning status—she was treading through the empty corridors towards the museum's entrance.

'Leaving so soon?'

The voice behind her on the wide stone staircase echoed in the otherwise deserted building, well away from the exhibition gallery.

This time she was more collected in her reaction. 'Yes,' she said.

'I'll drive you back,'

Anatole's footsteps quickened and he drew level with her. Moved to take her arm. She avoided it, stepping aside.

'Thank you, but my car is waiting.'

Hurriedly, she went out, stepped onto the wide pavement, thankful to see her chauffeured car at the kerbside.

She turned back to Anatole. He seemed taller than

ever, more overpowering. She lifted her chin. 'Don't let me keep you, Anatole,' she said.

It was nothing more than an expression, and yet she heard it echo savagely in her head. No, she had not been able to *keep* Anatole, had she?

Because I committed the cardinal sin in his book. The one unforgivable crime.

Her mind sheared away. Why remember the past? It was gone, and gone for ever.

She headed determinedly towards her car, but Anatole was there before her, opening her door. Then, to her consternation, as she got inside as quickly as her long gown permitted Anatole followed.

'I've dismissed my own car. I'll see you to your destination. Where are you staying?'

He realised he had no idea. Had Vasilis acquired a London base? He did not use his father's hotel suite— that he knew.

The suite I never went to that fatal night I took Tia into my arms—into my life.

No, don't remember that night. It was over, gone— nothing was left of that life now.

He heard her give with audible reluctance the name of a hotel. It was a top hotel, but a quiet one—not fashionable. Ideal for his uncle, Anatole acknowledged.

He said as much, and Christine nodded.

'Yes, Vasilis always liked it. Old-fashioned, but peaceful. And it has a lovely roof garden—you'd hardly know you were in London—'

She stopped. Memory sprang, unwanted, of Anatole's verdant roof terrace at his London apartment, of him saying that he did not care for cities.

There was a moment of silence. Was Anatole remembering too?

Well, what if he is? So what?

Defiance filled her, quelling the agitation that had leapt automatically as he'd got into the car. She was sitting as far away as possible, and even knowing the presence of Mr Hughes behind his glass screen was preventing complete privacy with Anatole, her heart was beating hectically. She tried to slow it—she must retain control, composure. She *must*!

I am Vasilis's widow. He can protect me still simply by virtue of that. That is my identity now.

She pulled her mind back—Anatole was speaking.

'I wanted to tell you,' he was saying, his voice stiff, as if the words did not come easily, 'how impressed I was with you tonight. You handled the occasion very well.' He paused. 'You did Vasilis proud.'

Christine's turned her head, her eyes widening. Had Anatole really just said that? Anatole who thought her the lowest of the low?

'I did it for him,' she said quietly, and looked away, out of her window, away from Anatole.

She could feel his presence in the car as something tangible, threatening to overpower her. How many times had she and he driven like this, through the city night? So many nights—so many cities...

It was so long ago—five years ago. A lifetime ago. And I am not the same person—not by any measure. Even my name is different now. I have been a wife, and now I am a widow—I am a mother. And Anatole can mean nothing to me any more. Nothing!

Just as she, in the end, had meant nothing to him.

Memory stabbed at her of how Anatole had sat her

down, talked to her, his face tense, the morning she had told him she wasn't pregnant after all.

'Tia—this is something you have to understand. I do not want to marry and I do not want to have children. Not with you—not with anyone. Now, if either or both of those things is something you do want,' he'd continued in the same taut voice, 'then you must accept that it is not going to happen with me. Not *voluntarily*.'

His voice had twisted on that word. He'd been sitting opposite her, leaning forward slightly, his hands hanging loosely between his thighs, an earnest expression on his face as if he were explaining something to someone incapable of understanding.

And that was me—I couldn't understand. So I learned the hard way....

He'd taken a breath, looked her straight in the eyes. 'I like you Tia. You're very sweet, and very lovely, and we've had a really great time together, but...' He'd taken another breath. 'What I will not tolerate is any attempt by you to...to get pregnant and force me to the altar. I won't have that, Tia—I won't have it.'

He'd held her eyes, making her hear what he was telling her.

'So from now on make sure there is no chance of another scare like this one, OK? No more getting "muddled up" over time zones.' And then an edge had come into his voice, and his eyes had had a look of steel in them. 'If that is what really happened.'

He'd got to his feet, his six-foot height dwarfing her seated figure, and she'd looked up at him, her throat tight and painful, her hands twisted in her lap.

'If you want a baby, Tia, accept that it cannot be

with me.' His expression had hardened. 'And if it's me you want one with—well, then you had better leave, right away, because it's over between us—*over.*'

He'd left the apartment then, heading to his office, and she'd watched him go. Her vision had grown hazy, and she'd felt feel sobs rising. The moment he'd gone she had rushed into the bathroom, releasing the pent-up tears, hating it that Anatole was being like that— hating it that she'd given him cause.

What she longed for so unbearably was what he did *not* want, and her heart felt as if it was cracking in pieces.

Her red-rimmed eyes had fallen on the little rect-angular packet by the basin. It had been delivered the day before but she had dreaded using it. Dreaded finding out. Finding out whether what she had once thought would be a dream come true was instead turn-ing into a nightmare. Was she forcing a child on Ana-tole—forcing him into a loveless, bitter marriage he did not want to make.

Then her period had arrived after all, making the test unnecessary.

She'd stared at the packet. Fear in her throat.

I've got to be sure—absolutely, totally sure—that I'm not pregnant. Because that's the only way he'll still want me.

She'd shut her eyes. She needed Anatole to want her on any terms at all. *Any* terms.

So she had done the test. Even though she hadn't needed to. Because she hadn't been able to bear not to.

She had done the test...and stared at the little white stick...

* * *

Christine's car was pulling up at the hotel. Anatole leant across, opening her door for her. The brush of his sleeve on her arm made her feel faint, and she had to fight to keep her air of composure, dangerously fragile as it was.

She turned to bid him goodnight. But he was getting out too. Addressing her.

'I need to speak to you.' He glanced at the hotel entrance. 'In private.'

He took her elbow, moved to guide her inside. Unless she wrested herself away from him, made a scene in front of Mr Hughes and the doorman tipping his hat to them, she must comply.

The moment she was indoors, she stepped away.

'Well?' she said, lifting her eyebrows, her expression still unyielding.

His eyes had gone to where a small bar opened up off the lobby, and she walked stiffly to one of the tables, sat herself down. The place was almost empty, and she was glad. She ordered coffee for herself and Anatole did likewise, adding a brandy.

Only when the drinks arrived did he speak. 'I've heard from Vasilis's London solicitors,' he opened.

Christine's eyes went to him. She was burningly conscious of him there—of his tall, effortlessly elegant body, of the achingly familiar scent of his aftershave, of the slight darkening of his jawline at this advanced hour of the evening.

How she had loved to rub her fingers along the roughening edges, feeling passion start to quicken...

Yet again, she hauled her mind away. Anatole's

voice was clipped, restrained as he continued. She realised he was tense, and wondered why.

'Now that probate has been granted they have told me the contents of Vasilis's will.' The words came reluctantly from him, his mouth tight. His eyes rested on her face, looking at her blankly. Then his expression changed. 'Why did you let me think you would inherit all my uncle's personal fortune for yourself?'

Christine's eyes widened. 'I didn't,' she said tightly. '*That*, Anatole,' she added, her voice sharp, 'was something you assumed entirely on your own!'

He half lifted his hand—as if her objection were irrelevant. As if there were more he had to say.

'My uncle's wealth has been left entirely in trust for his son—you get only a trivial income for yourself. Everything else belongs to Nicky!'

Her eyes flickered and her chin lifted. 'I wouldn't call my income *trivial*. It's over thirty thousand pounds a year,' she replied.

'Chickenfeed!' he said dismissively.

Her expression tightened. 'To you, yes. To me it's enough to live on if I have to—more than enough. I was penniless when I married Vasilis—as you reminded me. Of *course* everything must go to Nicky. And besides—' she allowed a flash of cynicism to show in her eyes '—as I'm sure you will point out to me, I will continue to reap the benefits of Nicky's inheritance while he's a minor. I get to live in a Queen Anne country house, and I'll have all of Nicky's money to enjoy while he grows up.'

A hand lifted and slashed sideways. 'But you will have no spending money other than your own income.'

Her composure snapped. 'Oh, for heaven's sake,

Anatole. What am I going to spend money on? I have enough clothes to last me a lifetime. And I've told you I have no ambition to racket around the world causing scandals, as you so charmingly accused me of wanting to do. I simply want to go on living where I do now— for my sake as much as Nicky's. It's where he's grown up so far, where I have friends and know people who knew Vasilis and liked him, valued him. If I want to take Nicky on holiday, of course funds will be made available to me. I shall want for nothing—though I'm sure you'll be the first to accuse me of the opposite!'

She saw him reach for his brandy, take a hefty mouthful before setting it down on the table with a decisive click.

'I can accuse you of nothing.' He took a breath— a deep, shuddering breath—and focussed his eyes on her. Emotion worked in his face. 'Instead—' He stopped, abruptly. His expression changed. So did his voice. 'Instead,' he repeated, 'I have to apologise. I said things to you that I...that were unfair—'

He broke off again. Reached for his coffee and downed it. Then he was looking at her again. As if she were not the person he had thought her to be.

But she isn't. She's not the avaricious, ambitious gold-digger I thought. It was she who insisted on Vasilis leaving his personal fortune to Nicky, his lawyers told me, with nothing for her apart from that paltry income.

It was not what he'd expected to hear. But because of it...

It changes everything.

It was the same phrase that had burst from him when he'd discovered the existence of Vasilis's son,

and now it burned in his head again, bringing to the
fore the second thing he had to tell her. The imperative that had been building up in him, fuelled by that
strange, compelling emotion that had filled him when
he'd crouched down beside the little boy to console
and comfort him.

'I would like to see Nicky again—soon.'

Immediately Christine's face was masked.

'He is my blood,' he said tightly. 'He should know
me. Even if—' He stopped.

She filled the gap, her face still closed. Her tone
was acid. 'Even if *I* am his mother?'

Anatole's brows drew together in a frown. 'I did
not mean—' Again he broke off.

He'd just told her he couldn't accuse her of wanting her husband's fortune—but she'd still persuaded a
man thirty years older than her to marry her in order
to acquire the lavish lifestyle she could never have
achieved otherwise. That alone must condemn her.
What other interpretation could there be for what she
had done when she had left him to marry his uncle?

Conflict and confusion writhed in him again.

'Yes, you did,' Christine retorted, her tone still acid.
'Anatole, look—try to understand something. *You* may
not have wanted to marry me, to have a child with
me—but your uncle did. It was his *choice* to marry
me. You insult him if you think otherwise and your
approval was not necessary.'

She saw his hand clench, emotion flash across his
face, but she didn't want to hear any more. She got to
her feet, weariness sweeping over her. She longed for
Vasilis's protective company, but he was gone. She

was alone in the world now. Except for Nicky—her beloved son.

The most precious being in the universe to her.

The very reason she had married.

Anatole watched her walk out—an elegant, graceful woman. A woman he had once held in his arms, known intimately—and yet now she was like a stranger. Even the name she insisted on calling herself emphasised that.

Emotion roiled within him in the confusing mesh that swirled so confusingly in his head, that he could make no sense of.

But there was one thing he *could* make sense of.

Whatever his conflicting thoughts about Tia—or Christine, as she now preferred to be known—and whatever she had done...abandoning him, marrying his uncle, remaking her life as Vasilis's oh-so-young wife...she'd gone up in the world in a way that she could never have imagined possible the day she had trudged down that London street with a heavy suitcase holding all her possessions.

Now she was transformed into a woman who was poised and chicly dressed, who was able—of all things!—to introduce an exhibition of ancient artefacts as if she were perfectly well acquainted with such esoteric knowledge. Yes, whatever she had done in these years when he had never seen her, there was one thing he could make sense of.

Nicky. The little boy who had lost the man he'd thought of as his grandfather—who would now be raised only by his mother, knowing nothing of his paternal background or his heritage.

Anatole's face steeled. Well, he would ensure that did not happen. He owed it to Vasilis—to the little boy himself—to play *some* part in his life at least.

A stab of remorse—even guilt—pierced him. In the five long years since Tia had left him he'd received, from time to time, communications from his uncle. Careful overtures of reconciliation.

He'd ignored them all—blanked them.

But he could not—*would* not—ignore the existence of Vasilis's young son.

I want to see him again!

Resolve filled him. Something about the child called to him.

Again that memory filled his head of how he'd distracted the little boy, talking about painting a picture of a train, just as he himself had once done for his uncle in that long-ago time when it had been he himself who'd been the child without any kind of father figure in his life to take an interest in him. When there had only been occasional visits from Vasilis—never his own father, to whom he had been of no interest at all.

Well, for Nicky it would not be like that.

He'll have me. I'll make sure of it!

And if that meant seeing Tia—Christine—again, well, that was something he would have to endure.

Unease flickered in him. *Can I cope with that? Seeing her in the years to come with Nicky growing up?*

It was a question that, right now, he did not want to think about.

CHAPTER SEVEN

'MUMMA, *LOOK*!'

Nicky's excited voice called to her and Christine finished her chat to Nanny Ruth and paid attention to her son.

They were out in the garden now that spring was here, and Nicky was perched on a bench beside a rangy young man who was showing him photos on his mobile phone.

As Nanny Ruth went off to take her well-earned break Christine went and sat herself down too, lifting Nicky onto her lap. 'What have you got there, Giles?' she asked with a smile.

The young man grinned. 'Juno's litter,' he said. 'They arrived last night. I couldn't wait to show Nicky.'

'One of them is going to be mine!' Nicky piped up excitedly. 'You said, Mumma, you *said*!'

'Yes, I did say,' Christine agreed.

She'd talked it through with Giles Barcourt and his parents. They were the village's major landowners from whom Vasilis had bought the former Dower House on the estate. They had always been on very friendly terms, and now, they were recommending to Christine that acquiring a puppy would help Nicky recover from losing his beloved *pappou*. She was in full agreement, seeing just how excited he was at the prospect.

'So,' Giles continued, 'which one shall it be, do you think? It will be a good few weeks before they're ready to leave home, but you can come and visit them to make your final choice.'

He grinned cheerfully at Nicky and Christine, and she smiled warmly back. He was a likeable young man—about her own age, she assumed, with a boyish air about him that she suspected would last all his life. He'd studied agriculture at Cirencester, like so many of his peers, and now ran the family estate along with his father. A born countryman.

'By the way,' he went on, throwing her a cheerful look again, 'Mama—' he always used the old-fashioned moniker in a shamelessly humorous fashion '—would love you to come to dinner next Friday. My sister will be there, with her sproglets and the au pair, so Nicky can join the nursery party. The sproglets are promised one of the pups too, so there'll be a bunfight over choosing. What do you say?'

Christine smiled, knowing the invitation was kindly meant. It would be poignant to be there without Vasilis. But at some point she must start socialising again, and the Barcourts had always been so kind to her. And Nicky would love it.

'That would be lovely—thank you!' she exclaimed, and Giles grinned back even more warmly.

She was aware that he was probably sweet on her—as he might have called it, had any such introspection occurred to him—but he never pushed it.

'Great!' he said. 'I'll let her know.'

He was about to say something else, but at that moment there was the sound of footsteps on the gravel path around the side of the house. She looked up, startled.

A mix of shock and dismay filled her. 'Anatole...' she said faintly.

This time there had not even been any warning from her housekeeper. Anatole must have parked his car, heard voices, and come across the gardens. Now he was striding up to them. Unlike last time he was not in a black business suit, nor in a tuxedo as he had been in London. This time he was wearing jeans, a cashmere sweater and casually styled leather jacket.

He looked...

Devastating.

A thousand memories drummed through her head, swooping like butterflies. Like the butterflies now fluttering inside her stomach as he stood, surveying the group. Her grip was lax suddenly, and she felt Nicky wriggle off her lap.

Excitement blazed from Nicky's face and he rushed up to Anatole. 'You came—you *came*!' he exclaimed. 'I did that painting! I painted it for Pappou, like you said.'

Anatole hunkered down. 'Did you?' He smiled. 'That's great. Will you show it to me later?'

There was something about the ecstatic greeting he was receiving that was sending emotion coursing through him. His grin widened. How could he possibly have stayed away so long when a welcome like this was coming his way?

'Yes!' cried Nicky. 'It's in my playroom.' Then something even more exciting occurred to him. 'Come and see my puppy!'

He caught at Anatole's hand, drew him over to the bench where Giles had got to his feet.

'Puppy?' queried Anatole.

He was focussing on Nicky, but at the same time he was burningly conscious of Tia's presence. Her face was pale, her expression clearly masked. She didn't want him there—it was blaring from her like a beacon—but he didn't care. He wasn't here for *her*, but for Vasilis's son. That was his only concern.

Not the way that her long hair was caught back in a simple clip...nor how effortlessly lovely she looked in a lightweight sweater and jeans.

Was her blonde loveliness the reason her current visitor was there? Anatole's eyes snapped across to the young man who'd stood up, and was now addressing him.

'Giles Barcourt,' he said in an easy manner, oblivious to what Christine instantly saw was a skewering look from Anatole. 'I'm a neighbour. Come to show young Nicky Juno's pups.' He grinned, and absently ruffled Nicky's hair.

Christine saw Anatole slowly take Giles's outstretched hand and shake it briefly.

'Giles—this is...' she swallowed '...this is Vasilis's nephew, Anatole Kyrgiakis.'

Immediately Giles's expression changed. 'I'm sorry about your uncle,' he said. 'We all liked him immensely.'

There was a sincerity in his voice that Christine hoped Anatole would respect. She saw him give a tight nod.

'Thank you,' he said.

His glance moved between her and Giles assess-

a past that never happened. Anatole did not want a child...did not want a child by me...did not want me for a wife...

Emotion rose up inside her in a billowing wave of pain. Pain for the idiot she'd been, her head stuffed full of silly fairytales!

With a cutting breath, she headed downstairs into her sitting room to phone the White Hart, and then let Mrs Hughes know they might have an unexpected guest for dinner. Her thoughts ran on—hectic, agitated.

She rubbed at her head. If only Anatole would go away. He'd kept away while Vasilis was alive. As if she were poison...contaminated. But if he was set on seeing Nicky—who seemed so thrilled that he'd come, so animated and delighted...

How can I stop Anatole from visiting, from getting to know Nicky? How can I possibly stop him?

She couldn't think about it—not now, not here.

With a smothered cry she made her phone call, put her housekeeper on warning, then got out the file on Vasilis's foundation and busied herself in the paperwork.

It was close on an hour later when the house phone went. It was Nanny Ruth, back on duty for the evening, wanting a decision about Nicky's teatime.

'Well, why not let him stay up this evening?' Christine said. That way, if Anatole was assuming he would dine here, she would have the shield of her son present. Surely that would help, wouldn't it?

Some twenty minutes later her housekeeper put her head round the door.

'Nicky and Mr Kyrgiakis are coming downstairs,' she said, 'and dinner's waiting to be served.'

Christine thanked her and got up. She would not bother to change. Her clothes were fine. Anatole would still be in his jeans and sweater, and Nicky would be in his dressing gown.

She went into the dining room, saw them already there. Anatole was talking to Nicky about one of the pictures on the wall. It was of skaters on a frozen canal.

'Brrr! It looks freezing!' Anatole was shivering exaggeratedly.

'It's Christmas,' explained Nicky. 'That's why it's snowy.'

'Do you have snowy Christmases here?' Anatole asked.

Nicky shook his head, looking cross. 'No,' he said disgustedly.

Anatole looked across at Christine, paused in the doorway. 'Your mother and I had a snowy Christmas together once—long before you were born, Nicky. Do you remember?'

If he'd thrown a brick at her she could not have been more horrified. She was stunned into silence, immobility.

With not a flicker of acknowledgement of her appalled reaction, he went on, addressing her directly. 'Switzerland? That chalet at the ski resort I took you to? We went tobogganing—you couldn't ski—and I did a black run. We took the cable car up, I skied down and you came down by cable car. You told me you were terrified for me.'

She paled, opening her mouth, then closing it again.

He was doing it deliberately—he *had* to be. He was referring to that unforgettable Christmas she'd spent with him and the unforgettable months she'd spent with him—

'What's tobogganinning?' Nicky asked, to her abject relief.

Anatole answered him. He was glad to do so. Had he gone *mad*, reminding Tia—reminding himself—of that Christmas they'd spent in Switzerland?

I'm not here to stir up the past—evoke memories. It's the future that is important now—the future of Vasilis's son. Only that.

He answered the little boy cheerfully. 'Like a sledge—you sit on it, and it slides down the hill on the snow. I'll take you one day. And you can learn to ski, too. And skate—like in the picture.'

'I like that picture,' Nicky said.

'It's worth liking,' Anatole said dryly, his eyes flickering to Christine. 'It's a minor Dutch Master.'

'Claes van der Geld,' Christine said, for something to say—something to claw her mind out of the crevasse it had fallen into with the memory of that Christmas with Anatole.

They'd made love on Christmas Eve, on a huge sheepskin rug, by the blazing log fire...

Anatole's eyes were on her, with that same look of surprise in them, she realised, as when she'd mentioned Vasilis discussing Aeschylus and Pindar with the vicar.

She gave a thin smile, and then turned her attention to Nicky, getting him settled on his chair, then taking her own place at the foot of the table. Anatole's place had been set opposite Nicky. The head of the table was empty.

As she sat down she felt a knifing pang in her heart at Vasilis's absence, and her eyes lingered on the chair her husband had used to sit in.

'Do you miss him?'

The words came from Anatole, and she twisted her head towards him. There was a different expression on his face now. Not sceptical. Not ironic. Not taunting. Almost...quizzical.

Her eyes narrowed. 'What do you think?' she retaliated, snatching at her glass, and then realising it had no water in it.

He reached for the jug of water on the table, filled her glass and then his own. 'I don't know,' he said slowly. His mouth tightened. 'There's a lot I don't know, it seems. For example...' his tone of voice changed again '... I didn't know that you knew about Dutch Old Masters. Or anything about Hellenistic sculpture. Or classical Greece literature. And yet it seems you do.'

She levelled a look at him. There was no emotion in it. 'Your uncle was a good teacher,' she said. 'I had nearly five years of personal tuition from him. He was patient, and kind, infinitely knowledgeable, and—'

She couldn't continue. Her voice was breaking, her throat choking. Her eyes misted and she blinked rapidly.

'Mumma...?'

She heard Nicky's voice, thin and anxious, and shook her unshed tears away, making herself smile and reach for her son, leaning forward to drop a kiss on his little head.

'It's all right, darling, Mumma's fine now.' She made her face brighter. 'Do you think Mrs H has made pasta?' she asked. It was no guess—Mrs Hughes always did pasta for Nicky when he ate downstairs.

'Yes!' he exclaimed. 'I *love* pasta!' he informed his cousin.

Anatole was grinning, all his attention on Nicky too. 'So do I,' he said. 'And so,' he said conspiratorially, 'does your mumma!'

His gaze slid sideways. He was speaking to her again before he could stop himself. Why, he didn't know. He only knew that words were coming from him anyway.

'We always ate it when you cooked. Don't you remember?'

Again, she reeled. Of *course* she remembered!

I remember everything—everything about the time we spent together. It's carved into my memory, each and every day!

She reached for her water, gulping it down. Then the door opened and Mrs Hughes came in, pushing a trolley.

'Pasta!' exclaimed Nicky in glee as Christine got to her feet to help her housekeeper serve up.

Nicky did indeed have pasta, but for herself and Anatole there was more sophisticated fare: a subtly flavoured and exquisitely cooked ragout of lamb, with grilled polenta and French beans.

There was no first course—Nicky wouldn't last through a three-course meal and he was eager to start eating straight away—but, again, Nanny Ruth's training held fast.

Christine put a few French beans on a side plate,

arranging them carefully into a tower to make them more palatable.

'How many beans can you eat?' she asked Nicky, and smiled. 'Can you eat ten? Count them while you eat them,' she said, draping his napkin around his neck—she knew Mrs Hughes's pasta came with to-mato sauce.

She turned back to put more dishes on the table, only to see Mrs Hughes lift two bottles of red wine and place them in front of Anatole.

'I've taken the liberty,' she announced, 'of bring-ing these. But of course there is all of Mr K's cellar if you think these won't do—that's why I haven't opened them to breathe. I hope that's all right with you?'

Christine said nothing, but bitter resentment welled up in her. Mrs Hughes was treating Anatole as if he were the man of the house. Taking her husband's place. But she said nothing, not wanting to upset her.

Nor, it seemed, did Anatole. 'Both are splendid,' he said approvingly, examining the labels, 'but I think this one will be perfect.' He selected one, handed back the other. 'Thank you!'

He cast her his familiar dazzling smile, and Chris-tine could see its effect on her housekeeper.

Mrs Hughes beamed. 'Good,' she said. Then she looked at Christine. 'Will Mr Kyrgiakis be staying to-night? I can make up the Blue Room if so—'

Instantly Christine shook her head. 'Thank you, but no. My husband's nephew has a room reserved at the White Hart in Mallow.'

'Very well,' said Mrs Hughes, and took her leave.

Christine felt Anatole's eyes upon her. 'Have I?' he enquired.

'Yes,' she said tightly. 'I reserved it for you. Unless you're driving back to town tonight, of course.'

'The White Hart will do very well, I'm sure,' replied Anatole.

His voice was dry, but there was something in it that disturbed Christine. Disturbed her a lot.

She turned to Nicky. 'Darling, will you say Grace for us?'

Dutifully, Nicky put his hands together in a cherubic pose. 'Thank you, God, for all this lovely food,' he intoned. Then, in a sing-song voice he added, 'And if we're good, God gives us pud.' He beamed at Anatole. 'That's what Giles says.'

Anatole reached for the foil cutter and corkscrew, which Mrs Hughes had set out for him, and busied himself opening the wine, pouring some for Christine and himself. Nicky, he could see, had diluted orange juice.

'Does he, now?' he responded. Wine poured, he reached for his knife and fork, turning towards Christine, who had started eating, as had Nicky—with gusto. 'This dinner party next Friday...tell me more.'

'There isn't much to tell,' she replied, keeping her voice cool.

She hadn't missed the dry note in Anatole's voice. But she didn't care. Let him think what he would about her friendship with Giles Barcourt. He would, anyway, whatever she said. She was condemned in his eyes and always would be.

'Don't expect a gourmet meal—but do expect hospitality. The Barcourts are very much of their type—landed, doggy and horsy. Very good-natured, easy-going. Vasilis liked them, even though they are completely oblivious to the fact that their very fine Gainsborough portraits of a pair of their ancestors need a thorough cleaning. He offered to undertake it for them, but they said that the sitters were an ugly crew and they didn't want to see them any better. Their Stubbs, however,' she finished, deadpan, 'is in superb condition. And they still have hunters in their stable that are descended from the one in the painting.'

Anatole laughed.

It was a sound Christine had not heard for five long years, and it made a wave of emotion go through her. So, too, did catching sight of the way lines indented around his sculpted mouth, the edges of his dark, gold-flecked eyes crinkled.

She felt her stomach clench and her grip on her knife and fork tighten. She felt colour flare out along her cheeks. Memory, like a sudden kaleidoscope of butterflies, soared through her mind. Then sank as if they'd been shot down with machine gun fire.

'I look forward to meeting them.' His eyes rested on Christine. His tone of voice changed. Hardened. 'Giles Barcourt would not do for you,' he said. 'As a second husband.'

She stared. Another jibe—coming hard at her. Dear God, how was she to get through this evening if this was what he was going to do? Take pot-shots at her over everything? Wasn't that what she'd feared? That his blatant animosity towards her would start to poison her son?

'I am well aware of that,' she said tightly. She took a mouthful of wine, needing it. Then she set it back, stared straight at Anatole. 'I am also well aware,

Anatole…' she kept her voice low, and was grateful that Nicky was still enthusiastically polishing off his plate of pasta, paying no attention to anything but that '…that I am not fit to be the wife of a man whose family have owned a sizeable chunk of the county since the sixteenth century!'

'That's not what I meant!' Anatole's voice was harsh, as if he were angry.

His expression changed, and Christine saw him take a mouthful of wine, then set the glass down with a click on the mahogany table. 'I meant,' he said, 'that your years with Vasilis have…have *changed* you, Tia—Christine,' he amended. He frowned, then his expression cleared. 'You've changed almost beyond recognition,' he said.

'I've grown up,' she answered. Her voice was quiet, intent. 'And I am a mother.' Her gaze went to Nicky. 'He gives my life meaning. I exist for him.'

She could feel Anatole's eyes resting on her. Feel them like a weight, a pressure. She saw him ready himself to speak.

But then, with an exaggerated sigh of pleasure, Nicky set down his miniature knife and fork and announced, 'I'm finished!' He looked hopefully at his mother. 'Can I have my pudding now? Is it ice cream?'

'*May* I,' corrected Christine automatically, her voice mild. 'And, yes, I expect so. But you'll have to wait a bit, your…your cousin and I are still eating.'

Had she hesitated too much on the word cousin? She hoped not.

'It's odd to think of myself as Nicky's cousin,' Anatole commented. 'When I'm old enough to be his—'

He stopped abruptly. Between them the unspoken

word hung like a bullet in mid-air. He reached for his wine, drank deeply, poured himself another glass. Emotion clenched in him, but he would not give it room.

Yet his eyes went back to Vasilis's son.

The son who could have been his if—

No, don't go there. It didn't happen. Accept it. And the fact that it did not was what you wanted.

His mouth tightened, eyes hardening. But by the same token it was what Tia *had* wanted. And because she hadn't been able to get it from him—well, she'd gone and got it from his uncle.

In his head, he heard Christine's words.

You may not have wanted to marry me, to have a child with me—but your uncle did! It was his choice to marry me—

He felt his mind twist. Could it possibly be *true*? Could his lifelong bachelor uncle actually have *wanted* a child? A son?

But even if that *were* true, why take someone like Tia for a wife—of all women! His own nephew's ex-lover—thirty years his junior! If he'd wanted a wife there would have been any number of women in their own social circle, of their own nationality, far closer to him in age, and yet still young enough for child-bearing.

His eyes went to Christine.

She'd trapped him. It was the only explanation. She'd played on his good nature, his kindness— evoked his pity for my spurning of her, of what she wanted from me.

His mind twisted again, coming full circle. What did it matter now how Tia had got his uncle to marry her? All that was important to him now was the little boy sitting there, who was going to have to grow up without a father. Without the father he should have had.

A loving, protective father who would have devoted himself to his son, made him centre stage of his life, the kind of father that every boy deserved...

Thoughts moved in his head, stirred by emotions that welled up from deep within. He lifted his wine glass, slowly swirled the rich, ruby liquid as if he could see something in those depths. Find answers to questions he did not even know he was asking—knew only that he could not answer them. Not yet.

His eyes lifted, went to the woman at the foot of the table. Her attention was not on him, but on her son, and Anatole felt emotion suddenly kick through him. Gone was the strained, stiff expression she always had on her face when he himself was talking to her, as if every moment in his company was an unbearable ordeal. Now, oblivious of him, she was talking to her little boy, and her expression was soft, her eyes alight with tender devotion.

Once, it was me she looked at like that—

His gaze moved over her, registering afresh her beauty, her youthful loveliness now matured. A beauty that would be wasted unless she remarried.

Instantly the thought was anathema to him. Urgently he sought reasons for his overwhelming rejection of Tia remarrying—or even having any future love-life at all. Sought them and found them—the obvious ones.

I won't have Vasilis's fatherless son enduring a stranger for a stepfather. Worse, a succession of

*'uncles'—Tia's lovers!—parading in and out of his
life. Let alone any who crave to share in the wealthy
lifestyle that Nicky will have as he grows up—that a
stepfather could have too, courtesy of Tia. And Tia
could take up with anyone! Anyone at all!*

Even if it was some upper-class sprig like Giles
Barcourt—there was no harm in a man like that—
he'd never make a good husband for Tia...not for the
woman she'd become. And besides—another thought
darkened his mind,—any man she married would want
children of his own, children who would displace
Nicky. Yet it was impossible to think she could live
in lonely widowhood for ever. She was not yet thirty!

His eyes went to her again, drawn to rest on her as
she talked to her son. *Thee mou*, how beautiful she
was! How exquisitely lovely—

Emotion kicked again. Something was forming in
his mind, taking shape, taking hold. Yes, she would
marry again. It was inevitable. Unavoidable. But no
stranger that she married could be the father that
Nicky needed. No *man* could be the father that Nicky
needed.

Unless...

From deep within, emotion welled. In the flickering synapses of his brain currents flowed, framing
the thought that was becoming real, forcing its way
into his consciousness. There was only one man who
could be the father Nicky needed. One obvious man...

Nicky was all but falling asleep as he polished off his
ice cream, and Christine abandoned her slice of *tarte
au citron* to go and lift him up, carry him to bed. But

Anatole was been there before her, effortlessly hefting Nicky into his arms.

Christine followed them upstairs, her face set. It was hard—*very* hard—to see Anatole carry Nicky so tenderly, so naturally.

Into her head sounded those bleak words he'd spoken to her that final harrowing morning.

'I don't want to marry and I don't want children.'

Her face twisted. Well, maybe a young cousin was different. Maybe that was OK for Anatole.

Something rose in her throat, choking her. An emotion so strong she could not bear it.

As she settled her son into bed, kissed him goodnight, Anatole stepped forward, murmuring something to him in Greek. Christine recognised it as a night-time blessing, and felt her throat tighten with memory. It was what Vasilis had said to bless his son's sleep.

And his son had recognised it too. 'That's what my *pappou* says,' Nicky said drowsily. His little face buckled suddenly. 'I want my *pappou*,' he cried, his voice plaintive.

Instinctively Christine stepped forward, but Anatole was already sitting himself down beside Nicky, taking his hand.

Anatole thought how strange it was to feel the feather-light weight of this cousin of his, to feel the warmth of his little body, to feel so protective of him.

It isn't his fault that he is now bereft, he thought. *Or that his mother inveigled Vasilis into marrying her. None of that is his fault. And if it was truly Vasilis's choice—however bizarre, however unlikely that seems—to marry Tia, then my responsibility to my uncle's child is paramount!*

But *was* it just a case of responsibility? That sounded cold, distant. What he felt for this little boy was not cold or distant at all—it welled up in him... an emotion he'd never felt before. Never known before. Strong and powerful. Insistent.

'How about if you had me instead, Nicky?' he said, carefully choosing his words, knowing he absolutely must get this right. 'How about,' he went on, 'if your *pappou* had asked *me* to look after you for him? Would that do?'

Dark, wide, long-lashed eyes stared up at Anatole. He felt his heart clench. He didn't know why, but it did. He stroked the little boy's hair, feeling his throat tighten unbearably.

'Yes, please,' Nicky whispered. He gazed up at Anatole. 'Promise?'

'Promise,' Anatole echoed gravely. And it was more than a word. It had come from deep within him.

Yet even as the word echoed he wondered if it could really be true, after his own miserable childhood, that he could make such a promise? All his life he'd resolved never to tread this path—but here he was, dedicating himself to this boy who seemed to be calling to something inside him he had not known he possessed. Had always thought was absent from him.

He watched Nicky's face relax, saw sleep rushing upon him. 'Don't forget...' were his slurring last words.

'No,' Anatole said gravely, stroking the fine silky hair. 'I won't.'

He felt his heart clench once more. What was this

emotion coursing through him that he had never known he could feel?

A sharp movement behind him made him turn his head. Christine was turning down the night light so that it would give a soft glow, but not be so bright as to disturb. But her eyes were fixed on Anatole.

Anatole was sitting on Nicky's bed, stroking his hair. And she saw an expression on his face that put barbed wire around her throat.

I can't bear this—I can't... I can't—

She walked out of the room, went downstairs to the hall, pacing restlessly until Anatole drew level with her. She opened her mouth to tell him that he should go, but he spoke pre-emptively.

'Come back into the dining room—I need to talk to you.' His voice was clipped, yet it had an abstracted tone to it.

'Anatole, I want you to go now—'

He ignored her, striding back into the dining room. Christine could only follow. He sat himself down at his dinner place, indicating that she should sit down too.

As if it's his house, his dining room—

Protest rose in her throat, but she sat down all the same.

'Well?' she demanded. Her heart-rate was up, emotions tearing at her. Anatole was looking at her, his gaze veiled, but there was something in it that made her go completely still.

'You heard Nicky,' Anatole said. His voice was taut, but purposeful. 'You heard his answer to my question about taking over from his *pappou*. You *heard* it, Christine—heard him say, *"Yes, please."* Well...'

He took a breath, and she saw lines of tension around his mouth.

'That is what I am going to do.' His eyes flared suddenly, unveiled. 'I am going to take Vasilis's place in his life. I am going to marry you.'

CHAPTER EIGHT

HAD THE WORLD just tilted on its side? Had an earth-quake just happened? Her vision was blurred...her heart seemed to have stopped.

'What?'

The word shot from her like a bullet. A bullet that found its target in the blankness of Anatole's face.

'Are you *insane*?' she shot again.

He lifted a hand. It was a jerky movement, as if designed to stop more bullets. As if to silence her.

'Hear me out,' he said. 'It's the obvious solution to the situation!'

Christine's eyes flashed. It felt as if her heart had still not started beating yet. 'What *situation*?' she demanded. 'There *is* no situation! I am Vasilis's widow. He has left me *perfectly* well provided for and even more so his son—a son who will before long no longer be so sad at the loss of his *pappou* and who will grow up adored by me and protected by Vasilis's wealth. What on earth about that needs a *solution*?'

Anatole's expression shifted. Something moved in his eyes. But his words, when he spoke, were stony. 'Nicky needs a father. All children do. With Vasilis gone, irrespective of whether Nicky thought of him as his grandfather, another man must take the role he played in his son's life.'

His eyes rested on Christine, shifting in their regard.

'You are not yet thirty, Tia—Christine—and it is impossible to envisage you not remarrying at some point.' He lifted his hand again. 'I take back what I said,' he said stiffly, 'about your likely dissolute lifestyle as the wealthy widow of a deceased much older husband.'

He felt the fury of Christine's eyes hurling daggers on him, even for saying that, even with his stiff apology, but he kept on speaking. It was vital he do so. Imperative.

'But it *is* inevitable that you will remarry,' he persisted. Something flashed darkly in his eyes. 'That neighbour of yours, Barcourt, would be only too eager—or any other man! And I do not mean that as an insult. I mean it as a compliment, Christine.'

He gritted his teeth.

'I appreciate that you would never marry anyone who would not be a doting stepfather to Nicky. And Barcourt—I give him this freely—is clearly cut out to be an excellent father. But he would not, as I said, make a good husband for you.'

His eyes rested a moment on her, his face taut, his eyes implacable.

'I would,' he said.

He took an incised breath.

'I would make an excellent husband for you. Think about it…'

He leant forward a little, as if to give emphasis to what he was saying—what he had to say to make her hear. Accept what had forced its way into his head and now could not be banished.

Urgently, he forged on. 'I am the closest relative to Nicky on his father's side. I discount my own father. He would be as little interested in Nicky as he was in me,' he said scathingly.

Christine could hear something in his voice that for the first time since he had tilted the world sideways for her with what he had said, stopping the beating of her heart, shifted her to react. There had been dismissal in his voice, but something else too. Something that she recognised. Recognised because she herself had been possessed by it totally and absolutely five years ago.

Pain—pain at rejection…at not being wanted.

But Anatole was speaking still, making her listen to him.

'Who better to be a father to Nicky than myself—his closest blood kin? And who better to be your husband, Christine…' his voice changed suddenly, grew huskier '…than me?'

His eyes washed over her—she could feel it like a silken brush over her senses.

'Who better than me?' he said again, his voice lower, that brush across her senses coming again.

She felt fatal faintness drumming at her again. She desperately wanted to speak, but she was voiceless. Bereft of everything except the sensation of his gaze washing over her, weakening her, dissolving her.

She tried to fight it—oh, dear God, she tried! Tried to remember all the pain he'd caused her.

But his eyes were washing over her now as they had done so many times, so long ago.

'I *know* you, Tia,' he said now, and the name he'd always called her by came naturally to him...as naturally as the wash of his eyes over her. 'And you know me. And we both know how compatible we are.'

He took another breath.

'And now we're much more so. You have matured into this woman you have become—poised, elegant, able to hold your own in company that would have terrified you five years ago! Five years ago you were young and inexperienced. Oh, I don't just mean sexually...'

He'd said the word casually, but it brought a heat to Christine's cheeks she would have given a million pounds for them not to have, and she beat it back as desperately as she could,

'I mean in all the ways of the world.'

His eyes slipped away, stared out as if into the past, a frown folding his brow.

He spoke again—with difficulty now. 'I didn't want to marry you then, Tia. I didn't want to marry anyone. Not just you—anyone at all. There was no reason for me to marry, and many not to. But now...' His eyes came back to her, sweeping in like a beacon, skewering her helplessly. 'Now there is every reason. To make a stable family for Nicky, a loving family—' He broke off, as if that had been hard for him to say.

For a moment Christine could not answer. Too much was pouring through her head—far, far too much. Then, with a scissoring breath, she said, 'I will not have a husband who despises me.'

It was tersely expressed, vehemently meant.

She saw him shake his head.

'I don't,' he answered. 'I don't despise you—'

Her eyes flashed blue fire. 'Don't lie to me, Anatole! You called me a cheap little adventuress! You thought me a scheming, ruthless gold-digger, who manipulated your hapless uncle into putting a wedding ring on my finger! And you thought I tried exactly the same thing on you—was perfectly prepared to get myself *pregnant*—' her mouth bit out the word as if it was rotten '—to make you marry me!'

His face turned stony. 'Whatever your motives for marrying Vasilis, I accept that you have not profited from his death and that you are devoted to your son.'

His eyes shifted again, and a troubled look drifted across them as a new thought formed—one that he had not had before. Had she wanted a baby so much that she'd been happy to marry a man so much older than her? Could it possibly be that it had not been his wealth that had made her marry his uncle? Had his riches *not* been the driving force behind her desire to marry Vasilis? Otherwise, why would she have insisted on not being the main beneficiary of his will?

He looked at her now—directly, eye to eye.

'Why did you marry my uncle?'

The strained look was instantly back in her face. 'I don't wish to discuss it. Think what you want, Anatole. I don't care.'

There was weariness in her voice, resignation.

With a jerking movement she got to her feet. 'It's time you left,' she said, her voice terse.

He stood also. Seeming to tower over her as Vasilis had never done.

Memory drummed in her, fusing the past with the present, making it impossible to separate them. Ramming home to her just how vulnerable she was to the man who stood there, a man who had always been able to melt her bones with a single glance from his deep, dark eyes. Who quickened her senses, heated the blood in her veins.

He wants to marry me—

The words were in her head—unbelievable, impossible. Yet they were there.

'You haven't given me your answer yet,' Anatole said.

His dark gaze was fixed on her. But this was the present, not the past. The past was over, would never return. *Could* never return.

With a summoning of her strength, she pulled herself together. 'I gave it to you instantly,' she countered. 'What you are proposing is insane, and I will treat it as such. And in the morning, Anatole, if you have any brain cells left in your head, you will agree with me.'

She walked out into the hall, moving to the front door, opening it pointedly.

He followed her out of the dining room. 'Are you really throwing me out of my uncle's house?' he said.

There was an edge in his voice that cut at her.

She pressed her lips together. 'Anatole, my husband was thirty years older than me. Do you think I haven't learnt to be incredibly careful about my reputation?' Her voice twisted. 'I know that my reputation can mean nothing to you, but for Nicky's sake have the decency to leave.'

He walked towards her. There was something in the way he approached her that made all the nerve fibres in her body quiver. Suddenly the space between them was charged with static electricity, flickering with lightning.

He looked at her speculatively. 'Do I tempt you, Tia?'

There was a caress in his voice, intimacy in the way his eyes washed over her. A caress and an intimacy that had once been as familiar to her as breathing. That she had not experienced for five long years. That was now alive between them again.

She could not breathe, could not move.

His hand reached for her and he drew one finger gently, oh-so-gently, down her cheek, brushing it across her parted lips. It felt like silk and velvet, and faintness drummed in her ears.

So long...it's been so long...

She felt her heart cry out his name, but it was from far away. Oh, so long ago. Echoing down the years to now—to this unbearable moment.

'You are more beautiful now than you ever were,' he said softly.

His eyes were holding hers, dissolving hers.

'How could I forget how beautiful you are? How could I not want you again, so incredibly beautiful, so very lovely...?'

She felt her body sway, had no strength to hold herself upright. It was as if all that was keeping her standing was his eyes, holding hers.

'So beautiful...' he murmured, his voice as soft as feathers.

Slowly, infinitely slowly, his mouth descended and his lips touched hers, grazed hers, moved slowly across her sweet, tender mouth. She made no move, not one—could not...would not. Dared not...

He drew back, his eyes searching hers. 'Once, Tia, you would have melted into my arms.'

He smiled—a warm, embracing smile that crinkled

the corners of his eyes, that made her remember all that had once been between them.

With that single, long, casual finger he tilted up her chin. 'So tiny, so petite...' He smiled again. His expression changed. 'You'll melt for me again, sweet Tia.'

He let his finger drop, took a breath, gave another final smile. Of confidence...of certainty.

What he wanted was right—was obvious. It was absolutely what should happen between them. It was an impulse, yes, but it had been impulse that had made him pile her into his car that afternoon all those years ago, drive off with her, take her to his apartment... his bed.

And had he not done so she would not be here now—his uncle's widow, the mother of a fatherless child, a young boy who needed a loving father as every child needed one, as every child needed a loving mother too, who made their child the centre of their universe. That was what he could do for Nicky— his uncle's child. Forge for him a loving family, keep him safe in that love all through his childhood... All his life.

I did not have that. Nicky will.

He smiled again, seeing how everything would resolve itself. Nicky would have himself, Anatole, to raise him, and he would have Tia—recreated now as Christine. Once, marriage had seemed impossible to him—fatherhood out of the question. But now, as emotion swept up in him, he knew that everything had changed for ever.

The future was crystal-clear to him and it was centred on this woman—this woman who was back in his life. It made clear, obvious sense all round. His desire for her was stronger than it had ever been. Her mature beauty drew him now even more than her *ingénue* loveliness had moved him—on that count there could be no doubt.

He spoke again to her, his final words for this evening, his tone a low, sensual husk, his eyes a caress.

'You'll melt, Christine,' he said, with promise in his voice, 'on our wedding night.'

Christine lay in bed, sleepless, her eyes staring up at the ceiling. Thoughts, emotions, confusion—all whirled chaotically around in her head. She could make sense of nothing. Nothing at all. Every now and then she would try and snatch at the whirling maelstrom, to try and capture it, but it always eluded her. Fragments skimmed past her again, just out of range.

He wants to marry me.

He despises me.

He kissed me.

None of it made sense—none of it—yet round and round the fragments whirled.

She tossed and turned, and found no rest at all.

But in the morning, when finally she awoke from the heavy, mentally exhausted slumber into which she'd fallen in the small hours, only one fragment was vivid in her head.

Temptation.

Oh, she could tell herself as much as she liked that it was insane that a man who had thrown the accusations at her that he had, a man who had told her to her face that he never wanted to marry her, should now be offering to do just that. Of his own free will.

It was insane that she should pay even the slightest attention to what he'd said. What he'd done. And yet tendrils of something writhed through her brain, finding soft, vulnerable places to cling to, to penetrate. She could feel it spreading in her mind…something so dangerous it terrified her.

Temptation.

Deadly, fatal temptation.

She had felt it once before—just as strong, just as dangerous. Once before she had been about to do something that with every instinct in her body she had known to be wrong. And the conflict had almost destroyed her. Would have destroyed her had it not been for Vasilis.

She had poured it all out to him that desperate day in Athens, when Anatole had made it so ruthlessly clear how little she meant to him—had set out the only terms under which he was prepared to continue with her, and what the consequences would be if she rejected those terms, broke them.

And Vasilis had listened. Had let her weep and sob and pour out all her misery and desperation. And then kindly, calmly and oh-so-generously, he had put forward another possibility for her.

He saved me. He saved me from the danger I was in of yielding to that overpowering temptation, that nightmare torment, that desperate desolation of realising that Anatole was a million miles away from what I yearned for.

Restlessly now, all these years later, she crossed to the window of her bedroom to look down over the gardens. She loved this house—this quiet, tranquil house that was so redolent of her marriage to Vasilis. He had brought her peace when her life had been in pieces.

Her eyes moved to the door set in the wall that led into a little dressing room, and from there into Vasilis's bedroom. A room that was now empty of him.

I miss him. I miss his kindness, his company, his wisdom.

Yet already, in the long months since she'd stood at his bleak graveside, he was beginning to fade in her head. Or perhaps it was not that he was fading, but that another was forcing himself into her consciousness. Into the space that had once been her husband's.

Just as her husband had once taken the space that had belonged to the man now replacing him.

I worked so hard to free myself of Anatole. Yet now he is back in my head, dominating everything.

And he was offering her now, with supreme, bitter irony, what he had never wanted to offer her before.

'Do I tempt you?'

Anatole had taunted her with those words and she had felt the force of them...the temptation to let herself be tempted. And then she had felt the touch of his mouth on hers...

With a smothered cry of anguish she whirled about, forcing herself to get on with the day—to put aside the insanity that Anatole was proposing, force it out of her head.

But when, mid-morning, she went up to Nicky's nursery to spend some time with him and let Nanny Ruth have a break, the first thing Nicky did was ask where Anatole was. She gave some answer—she knew not what—and was dismayed to see his little face fall.

Even more dismayed to discover that he remembered what he'd said so sleepily the night before. What Anatole had said.

His little face quivered. 'He said my *pappou* sent him to look after me. But where *is* he?'

She did her best to divert him, practising his reading and writing with him, until suddenly his eyes brightened and Christine, too, heard a car arriving—crunching along the front drive.

A bare few minutes later, rapid, masculine footsteps sounded outside, the nursery door opened, and there was Anatole.

With a whoop of glee Nicky rushed to him, to be swung up into Anatole's arms. Christine could only gaze at them, emotion scything inside her powerfully at the sight of her son's blazing delight at Anatole's arrival—and Anatole, his face softening, showed in every line of his body his gladness to see Nicky.

He turned to Christine, with Nicky held effortlessly in the crook of his arm, one little hand snaked around his neck, and the pair of them smiled broadly at her.

So like each other...

There was a humming in her ears, blood rushing, and she could only blink helplessly. Then Anatole was speaking...

'Who wants to go on an adventure today?' he asked.

Nicky's eyes lit up. 'Me! Me!' came the excited reply.

Anatole laughed and swung him down on his feet again, his eyes going to Christine.

'It's a glorious day out there—how about an outing? All three of us?'

She opened her mouth to give any number of objections, but in the face of Nicky's joyous response could not voice them. 'Why not?' she said weakly. 'I'll let Nanny know.'

She made her escape, finding Nanny Ruth in her sitting room, watching a programme about antiques on the TV and finishing off a cup of tea.

'What a good idea!' she said, beaming when Christine told her of Anatole's plans. She looked at her employer. 'It will distract Nicky. And, if I might say...' Christine got the impression that she was picking her works carefully '... I am very glad that young Mr Kyrgiakis is finally in touch.' She nodded meaningfully. 'He's clearly very fond of Nicky already. It will be important for Nicky to have him in his life.'

Her eyes never left Christine's and then she took a breath, as if having said enough, and got to her feet.

'Now, where does young Mr K plan on going today? I'll make sure Nicky has the right clothes.'

She headed into the playroom, leaving Christine feeling outmanoeuvred on all fronts. With deep misgiving she went downstairs, fetching a jacket for herself.

A whole day in Anatole's company—with only Nicky to shelter behind.

Tension netted her, and she felt her heart-rate increasing. She knew what was causing it to do so. Knew it and feared it.

CHAPTER NINE

'THIS,' ANNOUNCED NICKY with a happy sigh, 'is the best day *ever*!' He sat back in his chair, a generous smear of chocolate ice cream around his mouth.

Christine laughed—she couldn't help it. Just as she hadn't been able to help herself laughing when she'd realised just where Anatole was taking them.

'*A holiday camp?*' she'd exclaimed disbelievingly as they'd arrived in Anatole's car.

He'd somehow procured a child's booster seat, and Nicky had stared wide-eyed with dawning excitement as they parked.

'Day tickets,' Anatole had replied. He'd looked at Nicky. 'Do you think you'll like it?'

The answer had been evident for over six hours now. From the incredible indoor swimming paradise—towels and swimwear for all three of them having been conveniently purchased from the pool shop—with its myriad slides and fountains and any number of other delights for children, to the outdoor fairground, finishing off the day with a show based on popular TV characters.

Now they were tucking into a high tea of fish and chips and, for Nicky, copious ice cream. Christine leant forward to mop his face. Her mood was strange. It had been impossible not to realise that she was enjoying herself today. Enjoying, overwhelmingly, Nicky's excitement at everything. And Anatole's evident pleasure in Nicky's delight.

His focus had been on her little boy, and yet Christine had caught herself, time and time again, exchanging glances with Anatole over Nicky's expressions of joy at the thrills of the day. Brief glances, smiles, shared amusement—as the day had gone on they had become more frequent, less brief.

The tension that had netted her before they'd set off had evaporated in a way she could not have believed possible, and yet so it was. It was as if, she suddenly realised with a start, the old ease in his company, which had once been the way she was with him until the debacle that had ended their relationship, was awakening as if after a long freezing.

It was disturbing to think of it that way. Dangerous!

As dangerous as it had been when, emerging with Nicky from the changing rooms at the poolside, her eyes had gone immediately to Anatole's honed, leanly muscled form, stripped down to swim shorts. Memory had seared in her and she'd had to drag her eyes away. But not before Anatole had seen her eyes go to him—and she knew that his had gone to her.

Although she'd deliberately chosen, from the range available in the on-site shop, a very sporty swimsuit, not designed in the slightest to allure, consciousness of her body being displayed to him had burned in her as she'd felt his gaze wash over her.

Then, thankfully, Nicky, his armbands inflated, had

begun jumping up and down with eagerness to be in the water and the moment had passed.

That consciousness, however, resurfaced now as, tea finished and back in the car for their return journey, she realised that Nicky had fallen asleep, overcome with exhaustion after the day's delights. In the confined intimacy of the car, music playing softly, Anatole's presence so close to her was disturbing her senses.

She felt his eyes glance at her as he drove. Then he spoke. 'What I said last night—has today shown you how good it would be, making a family for Nicky?'

His tone was conversational, as if he'd asked her about the weather and not about the insanity of marrying him.

She was silent for a moment. Though it seemed to her that her heavy heartbeat must be audible to him, as it was to her. She tried to choose her words carefully. One of them had to be sane here—and it had to be her.

'Anatole, think about it rationally. You're running on impulse, I suppose. You've only just discovered about Nicky, and Vasilis is barely in his grave. For you—for *either* of us!—to make any kind of drastic alteration to our lives at such a time would be disastrous.' She looked at him. 'Everything I've read about bereavement urges not to take any major decisions for at least a year.'

Would that sufficiently deter him? She could only hope so. Pray so. Yet in the dimming light of the car she could see a mutinous look on his face. He was closing down—closing out what she'd said.

'It's the right thing to do,' he said.

There was insistence in his voice, and he could

hear it himself. How could she not see the obvious sense of what he was proposing? The rightness of it. Yes, he was being impulsive—but that didn't mean he was being irrational. In fact the very opposite! It was so clearly, unarguably right for him to make a family for this fatherless boy by marrying his mother— the very woman who'd once wanted a child by him... the woman he'd desired from the first moment he'd set eyes on her.

And I desire her still! And she desires me too. There is no doubt of that—no doubt at all!

Yet still she was denying it. As her blunt answer proved.

'No,' she answered. 'It isn't.'

Her head dipped, and she stared at her hands, lying in her lap. What more could she say without ripping apart the fragile edifice of her life—plunging herself back into the desperate torment she had once known with Anatole? The torment that had raked her between temptation and desolation?

She felt him glance at her. Felt the pause before he answered, with a tightness in his voice that she could not be deaf to.

'I'm not used to you disagreeing with me,' she heard him say. There was another pause. 'You've changed, Tia—Christine.'

Her head lifted, and she threw him a look. 'Of *course* I've changed,' she said. 'What did you expect?'

She took a breath that was half a sigh, remembering, for all her defiant words, how she'd used to love watching him drive, seeing how his hands curved so strongly over the wheel. How she'd drink in his profile, the keen concentration of his gaze. How she'd always loved gazing at him, all the time, marvelling over and over again at how wonderful, how blissful it was that he wanted her at all, how he had taken her by the hand and led her into the fantasy land where she'd dwelt with him…

He caught her eye now, and there was a glint in it that was achingly familiar.

'You used to gaze at me like that all the time, Tia. I could feel it, know it—sense it.'

His voice had softened, and though there was a trace of amusement in it there was also a hint of something she had not heard from him at all since the moment he'd stalked into her life again.

Tenderness.

She felt her throat catch and she dragged her eyes away, out over the road, watching the cars coming towards them, headlights on now as dusk gathered in the countryside.

'That was then, Anatole,' she said unsteadily. 'A long time ago—'

'I've missed it,' he answered her.

She heard him take a breath—a ragged-sounding one.

'I missed *you,* Tia, when you left me. When you walked out on me to marry my uncle, to become his pampered young bride.' There was an edge in his voice now, like a blade.

Her eyes flew to him, widening. '*I* didn't leave *you*!' she exclaimed. '*You* finished it with *me*! You told me you refused to have a relationship with someone who wanted to marry you, to get pregnant by you!'

She saw a frown furrow his brow, and then he threw a fulminating look at her, his hands tightening on the wheel. 'That didn't mean you had to *go*,' he re-taliated. 'It just meant—' He stopped.

'You just meant that I had to give up any idea of meaning anything to you at all—let alone as your wife or the potential mother of your children. Give up any idea of making a future with you!'

Christine's voice was dry, like sandpaper grating on bare skin. She shut her eyes for a moment, her head swirling, then opened them again, taking another weary breath.

'Oh, Anatole,' she said, and her voice was weary, 'it's all right. I get the picture. You were young, in the prime of your carefree life. I was an amusing diversion—a novelty! One that lasted a bit longer than you probably intended at first, when you scooped me off the road. I came from an entirely different walk of life from you—I was pretty, but totally naïve. I was so blatantly smitten by you that you couldn't resist indulging yourself—and indulging *me*. But I know that didn't give me any right to think you might want me long-term. Even if...'

She swallowed painfully, knowing she had to say it.

'Even if there hadn't been that pregnancy...scare...' she said the word with difficulty '...something else would have ended our affair. Because...' Her throat was tight. 'Because an affair was all it was. All it could ever be.'

She knew that now—knew it with the hindsight of her greater years. She had been twenty-three... Anatole had been the first man in her life—and a man such as she had never dreamt of, not even in her girl-ish fantasies! He'd taken her to fairyland—and even in her youthful inexperience she had feared that it would all be fairy gold and turn to dust.

And so it had. Painfully. Permanently.

'But now I want more,' he replied, and his words and the intensity of his voice made her eyes fly to him again. 'I want much, much more than an affair with you.'

He took a breath, changing gear, accelerating on an open stretch of road as if that would give escape to the emotion building up inside him. Emotion that was frustration at her obstinacy, at her refusal to concede the rightness of what he was proposing.

'Christine, this *works*—you, me and Nicky! You can see it that works. Nicky likes me, trusts me…and, believe me, I meant exactly what I said to him last night. That he can believe that his *pappou* sent me to look after him in his place. To become his father—'

He could have been my son! Had Tia been pregnant then—five years ago—Nicky would be my son. A handful of months older…no more.

Emotion rolled him over. Over and over and over— like a boulder propelled down a mountainside by an overwhelming, unstoppable force. Emotion about what might have been, about what had never been, that silenced him until they arrived at Vasilis's house—now Christine's home.

The home she kept for her son—his uncle's son— just as the legacy of Vasilis's work, his endless endeavours to preserve the treasures of the past, would pass to her guardianship.

And she will guard it well. How strange that I can trust her to do that, that I know now that I can trust her.

Yet it was not strange at all—not now that he had

seen her in London, at the exhibition opening, and here as chatelaine of this gracious house. She had grown into it—into a woman who could do these things, *be* these things.

Just as I have grown into what I am doing now. Accepting that I want a wife. A child.

He scooped up the sleeping boy, cradling his weight in his arms as he walked indoors with him. Christine opened the front door, leading the way upstairs in the quiet house—both Mrs Hughes and Nanny Ruth were out for the evening.

In his bedroom, they got Nicky into bed, still fast asleep, exhausted by the day's delights. For a moment, Anatole stood beside her as they gazed down at the sleeping child, illumined only by the soft glow of the night light.

His hand found Christine's. She did not take it away. She stood with him as they looked down at Nicky. As if they were indeed a family indeed…

Was there a little sound from her? Something that might have been a choke? He did not know. Knew only that she'd slipped her hand from his and was walking out of the room. He looked after her, a strange expression on his face, then back at Nicky, reaching almost absently to smooth a lock of dark hair from his forehead, to murmur a blessing on the night for him.

Then he turned and went downstairs.

Christine was waiting in the hall by the front door. Her head was lifted, her expression composed.

'Thank you for a lovely day,' she said.

She spoke calmly, quelling all the emotion welling up inside her. What use to feel what was inside her? It was of no use—it never could be now.

She opened the door, stepped back. He came up to her, feeling that strange, strong emotion in him again. This time he made no attempt to kiss her.

'It's been good,' he said.

His voice was quiet. His eyes steady. Then, with a quick smile, the slightest nod of his head, he was gone, crunching out over the gravel beneath the mild night sky.

As he opened his car door he heard the front door of the house close behind him.

Shut it, if you will—but you cannot shut me out. Not out of Nicky's life—or yours.

Certainty filled him as to the truth of that.

In the week that followed Christine did her best to regain the state of mind she'd had since her marriage to Vasilis. But it had gone—been blown away by the return of Anatole into her life. His invasion of it.

It was an invasion that had been angrily hostile, and he had been scathing in his denunciation of her behaviour. And the searing irony of it was that anger and hostility from him was so much easier for her to cope with. What she couldn't cope with—what she was pathetically, abjectly unable to cope with—was the way he was with her now.

Wooing!

The word stayed in her head, haunting her.

Disturbing her. Confusing her.

Changing her.

And she didn't want to change. She'd made a new life for herself—made it in tears and torment, but she was safe inside it. Safe inside the life Vasilis had given her. *That* was what she wanted to cling to.

Anatole is my past. I can't—I won't—have him as my future!

She dared not. Too much—oh, far too much—was at stake for her to allow that. More than she could bear to pay again.

Her resolve was put to the test yet again the following Friday—the day the Barcourts had invited her and Nicky over. Her hope that Anatole had forgotten proved to be in vain. He arrived in time to drive them over. And at the rambling Elizabethan mansion the Barcourts' welcome to Anatole could not have been friendlier.

'I'm glad you could come this evening, Mr Kyrgiakis. We were all so sorry to hear about your uncle—he was well liked, and very well respected.' Mrs Barcourt smiled kindly at Anatole as she greeted him, then led the way into the oak-panelled drawing room.

Nicky was scooped up by the nursery party, who were rushing off to see the puppies with the nanny, and Giles's sister Isabel, as cheerful as her brother, launched into a panegyric about the beneficial effects a puppy had on childhood, adding that Nicky should also learn to ride—as soon as he could. Giles agreed enthusiastically, volunteering their old pony, Bramble, for the job.

'Don't you agree?' Isabel said to Anatole.

'I'm sure my young cousin would love it,' he answered. 'But it is Christine's decision.'

He glanced at her and she smiled awkwardly. What the Barcourts were making of Anatole, she had no idea—knew only that they were asking no questions about him and seeming to take his presence for granted.

But her relief lasted only until after dinner, when their hostess announced they would leave the menfolk to their port and drew Christine and Isabel off to the drawing room. There, a bottle of very good madeira was produced, and Isabel went off to see her children.

Mrs Barcourt, Christine realised with dismay, was about to start her interrogation.

'My dear, *what* a good-looking young man! *Such* a shame we've seen nothing of him until now!' she exclaimed. She bent to absent-mindedly stroke the ancient, long-haired cat lounging on the hearth rug. 'I take it we'll be seeing a lot more of him now?'

Her smile was nothing but friendly. The question was clearly leading…

Christine clutched her glass. 'He *would* like to get to know Nicky,' she managed to get out.

Her hostess nodded sympathetically. 'Very understandable,' she said. 'And very good for Nicky too.' She paused. 'It's early days, I know, but you *will* need to think of the future, Christine—as I'm sure you realise.'

She stroked the cat again, then looked at her guest, her expression open.

'A stepfather would be excellent for Nicky—but you must choose wisely.' She made a face and spoke frankly, as Christine had known she would. 'Not Giles,' she said, with a little shake of her head. 'Fond though he is of Nicky, you wouldn't suit each other, you know.'

Christine's expression changed. 'No, no… I know that.'

Her hostess nodded. 'I know you do, my dear, and I'm glad of it.' She sat back, picking up her glass.

'You and Anatole seem to get on very well…' She trailed off.

Christine had no idea what to say, but Mrs Barcourt did.

'Well, I shall say no more except that I can see no reason not to look forward to getting to know him better. You must both come over again before long. Ah, Isabel—there you are!' she exclaimed as her daughter breezed in. 'How is little Nicky?'

'Begging for a sleepover, and my brood are egging him on! What do you say, Christine?'

Christine, abjectly grateful for the change of subject, could only nod. 'If you're sure it's no trouble?'

'Not in the least,' Isabel answered cheerfully. 'And tomorrow morning he can try out Bramble, if you're all right with that. Loads of kiddie riding kit here!'

Christine nodded weakly. But belatedly she realised that if Nicky slept here tonight she would be without his protective presence herself.

It was something she felt more strongly at the end of the evening, when she sat beside Anatole in his car, heading home.

He glanced at her. She'd looked enchanting all evening, wearing a soft dark blue velvet dress, calf-length in a ballerina style, with a double strand of very good pearls—presumably a gift from his uncle—and pearl ear studs. Her hair was in a low chignon, with pearl clips. Simple, elegant—and breathtakingly lovely.

Young Giles Barcourt had thought so too, Anatole thought, with an atavistic male instinct. Was that why he'd felt the need to make a point of emphasising his family link with Christine? Staking his claim to her?

Re-staking it.

She is mine. She's always been mine!

Certainty streamed through him. Possessiveness. Remorse and regret.

Why did I let her go—why did I not rush to her and claim her from Vasilis before he married her? Instead I gave in to anger and to my determination not to be forced into marriage and fatherhood.

Well, he hadn't been ready then—but he was ready now. More than ready. All he needed was to persuade Christine that he was right. And if words could not do so, then other means might.

He made some anodyne remark to her now—about the evening, about the pair of Gainsboroughs hanging in the dining room that Vasilis had itched to see cleaned—and said that he agreed with their hosts that perhaps they were best left covered in thick varnish. He had the gratification of hearing Christine chuckle, and then she asked if he'd spotted the very handsome Stubbs in pride of place over the fireplace.

'Indeed,' he replied. 'Do you think Bramble is one of the descendants?' It was a humorous remark, and intended to be so.

'I hope not!' Christine returned. 'That Stubbs stallion looks very fearsome!'

'Do you mind Nicky learning to ride?' Anatole asked as he steered the car along the dark country lanes back to the house.

She shook her head. 'I'm very grateful to Giles and Isabel,' she acknowledged. 'I want Nicky to grow up here, so riding will certainly make him feel at home. And he's very attached to Giles—'

The moment she spoke, she wished she hadn't. Even in the dim interior she could see Anatole's face tighten. She recalled Mrs Barcourt's words to her—not about her son, who was perfectly well understood between them, but about Anatole. Dear God, surely she and Anatole weren't coming across as a couple, were they? Please, *please* not! The very last thing she could bear was any speculation in that direction.

It was bad enough coping with the pressure from Anatole, let alone any expectations from the Barcourts. Consternation filled her about how she was going to handle Anatole's comings and goings—even if they were only to see Nicky. Talk would start—it was inevitable in a small neighbourhood. People would have them married off before she knew it.

Turmoil twisted in her, keeping her silent.

Anatole, too, was silent for the remainder of the short journey.

When they arrived back at her house she got out, preparing to bid him goodnight before he drove back to the White Hart. But instead he said, in a perfectly conversational voice, 'I could do with a nightcap. As the designated driver I got very little of that excellent claret over dinner—and none at all of the port that Barcourt Senior tried to press on me! So I could still have one more.' He glanced expectantly at Christine. 'He mentioned that he gave Vasilis a bottle at Christmas…'

Reluctantly, she let Anatole follow her inside. The house was very quiet—the Hugheses were in their apartment in the converted stables, and Nanny Ruth was away for the weekend. In the drawing room she switched on the table lamps, giving the elegant room a soft warm glow, and extracted the requisite bottle and two port glasses from a lacquered cabinet, setting them down with a slight rattle on a low table by the silk-upholstered sofa.

Anatole strolled across and seated himself, but Christine chose the armchair opposite, spreading her velvet skirts carefully against the pale blue fabric. He poured her a generous measure, and himself as well, then raised his glass to her. His gaze was speaking.

'To us, Christine—to what we can make together.'

His eyes held hers—dark, long-lashed, deep and expressive. She felt their power, their force. The long-ago memories they kindled within her. Emotion swirled, dark and turbid, troubling and disturbing.

It was as disturbing as feeling Anatole's lambent gaze upon her, which did not relinquish her as he took a mouthful of the sweet, strong, rich ruby port. She took a mouthful herself, needing its strength to fortify her.

The bottle had not been opened before—Vasilis's health had worsened steadily, remorselessly after Christmas, and he'd openly prepared her for the coming end. She felt her eyes blur with a mist of tears.

'What is it?' Anatole's voice was quiet, but she could hear the concern in it. 'You're not worrying about Nicky, are you?'

She shook her head. 'No—I'm used to leaving him for a night or two. He never fretted when I went to London with Vasilis.'

Her voice trembled over her late husband's name. Anatole heard the emotion in it and it forced a recognition in him. One he had held back for many years.

'You cared for him didn't you? My uncle?' he said. His voice was low. Troubled. As if he were facing something he didn't want to face. Something he'd held at bay for five long bitter, angry years.

'Yes—for his kindness,' she said feelingly. 'And his wisdom. His devotion to Nicky—'

She broke off. Thoughts moved within Anatole's mind—thoughts he did not want to think. His uncle—decades older than Tia and yet she'd had a child with him.

His mind blanked. It was impossible, just *impossible*, to envisage Nicky's conception. It was wrong to think of Tia with anyone else in the whole world except himself. Not his uncle, not young Giles Barcourt—no one!

The same surge of possessiveness he'd felt in the car swept over him again as his eyes drank her in, sitting there so close to him, looking so beautiful it made his breath catch.

How did I last this long without her?

It seemed impossible that he had. Oh, he'd not been celibate, but there had been only fleeting liaisons, deliberately selected for their brevity and infrequency. He'd put that down to having had such a narrow escape with Tia, when she'd so nearly trapped him into marriage—into unwanted fatherhood—exacerbating his existing resistance to women continually seeking to marry him. And yet now that he *did* want to marry her—the same woman who'd once dreamt of that very thing—she was refusing him.

Her words to him echoed in his head, giving him a reason for her obduracy that he could not accept. *Would* not.

'But that does not mean you cannot marry again!' he said.

Her gaze shifted away. 'Anatole—please. Please don't.'

Her voice was a thread. It was clearly unbearable to her that he should say such a thing. But he could not stop.

'Did he…care…for *you*?'

He did not like to think of it. It was…*wrong*. As wrong as Tia having feelings for a man who had probably been older than her own father, had he lived.

'He was fond of me,' she said. Her eyes went to him. 'And he adored Nicky.' She took a breath. 'That was what I valued most—that I was able to give him Nicky. He would never otherwise have had a child had he not married me.'

There was defiance in her voice, and Anatole knew the reason for it. Felt the accusation. Knew he had to answer it. That it was time to face what he had said, what he had done.

He took a breath—a difficult one—and looked her in the face, his expression sombre. 'I'm sorry, Christine. Sorry that when we were together I did not want a child. That I welcomed the fact you were not pregnant after all.'

He took a mouthful of port, felt it strong and fiery in his throat.

'I was not ready to be a father.' His eyes met hers. Unflinching. 'But now,' he said, 'I am. I want to be the father to Nicky that Vasilis did not live to be. I feel,' he swallowed 'I feel my uncle would want that. And I want so much for you to want it too.'

There was a choking noise from Christine and immediately Anatole was there, his port glass hastily set down, kneeling on the Aubusson carpet before Christine's chair, taking her hand. The mist of tears in her eyes was spilling into diamond drops on her lashes.

'Don't cry, Tia,' he said softly, lifting a finger to brush away the tears. 'Don't weep.'

His hand lifted the hand he was holding, which was trembling in his grasp, and he lifted it to his lips, smoothing his mouth across her knuckles.

'We can make this work—truly we can. Marry me— make things as right between us as they were wrong before. Make a family for your son with me—for his sake, for my uncle's sake. For my sake. For your sake.'

His eyes were burning into hers and she was gazing down into their depths, tears still shimmering. He took the half-empty glass from her trembling hand, then retained that hand, getting to his feet, drawing her with him. Light from the table lamp illumined her and his breath caught. How lovely she was...how beautiful.

His mouth lowered to hers. He could not stop— could not prevent himself. Desire streamed within him, and the memory of desire, and both fused together—the past into the present. Her lips were honey to his questing mouth, sweet and soft, and he felt arousal spring within him, strong and instant. His kiss deepened and he heard her make a low noise in her throat, as if she could not bear what was happening. As if she could not bear for him to stop.

His hands slipped from hers, sliding around her slender waist, pulling her gently, strongly, against him. He felt the narrow roundness of her hips against his. Felt his own arousal surge yet more. His blood coursed through him and he deepened his kiss as passion and desire drove him on.

She was quickening in his arms—he could feel it—

and he remembered, with a vividness that was like a flash of searing lightning, how she had always responded when he kissed her like this...how her slender body trembled, strained against him...how her eyes grew dazed as they were dazed now, with a film of desire glazing them as her pupils flared with arousal and the sweet peaks of her breasts strained against the wall of his chest.

He felt her nipples cresting, arousing him. She was kissing him back now—ardently, hungrily. As if she had not kissed anyone for a long, long time. As if only he could sate her hunger.

The last of his control broke. He swept her up into his arms. She was as light as a feather, as thistledown, and the soft material of her skirts draped over his thighs as he carried her from the room, up the wide sweep of stairs into the waiting bedroom. He laid her down on the bed, came down beside her.

How his clothes were shed he did not know—he knew only that her hair had been loosened from its pins and was spilling out upon the pillows, that he was parting the long zip of her dress and peeling it from her body so that her pale, engorged and crested breasts, so tender and so tempting, were exposed to him.

Memory knifed through him of all the times he had made love to her—to Tia, his lovely Tia—so soft in his arms, so yielding to his desire. And she was his again! His after so, *so* long. All that was familiar flooded back like a drowning tide, borne aloft by passion and desire, by memory and arousal.

His palm cupped her breast and he heard her moan again, low in her throat. The dazed look in her distended eyes was dim in the shadows of the night. His mouth lowered to her breast, fastening over her crested nipple, and his tongue worked delicately, delectably, around its sensitive contours.

The moan came again, more incoherent, and he felt her hands helpless on his back. Her neck was arched against the pillows, her throat exposed to him, and he drew his fingers down the length of it, stroking softly, holding her for himself as he moved his mouth to her other breast, to lave it with the same ministrations.

But her sweet ripened breasts were not enough. He wanted more. He felt a low, primitive growl, deep in his being.

He drew her dress from her completely, revealing tiny panties, slipping her free of them. Her thighs slackened and the dark vee between was a darker shadow. He propped himself on one elbow, taking her mouth with his again, feasting on it with slow, arousing sensuality, splaying his free hand on her soft pale flank.

He smiled down at her in the darkness. 'Tell me you do not want this. Tell me you do not want *me*,' he said to her. His voice was low. Driven. 'Tell me to go, Tia—tell me now, or do not tell me at all.'

It was impossible for her to give such an order. Her resistance was gone. How could it persist when his mouth, his hands, his tongue, his lips, his body and all his being were taking her where she should not be going, to what she should not be yielding to?

And yet she *was* yielding. Was succumbing hopelessly, helplessly, to what her body was urging her to do. It was taking her over, demolishing, drowning what her head was telling her. Her head was telling her that it was madness, insanity, to do what she was doing. But she could not stop. It was impossible to do so—impossible not to let the muscles of her thighs slacken, not to tighten her fingers over his strong, warm shoulder as delirium possessed her, as her body swept away the long, empty years since Anatole had last made love to her, had last taken her with him to that place only he could take her to. Where he was taking her again…now, oh, *now*!

She moaned again, her head starting to thresh, her spine arching, the muscles in her legs tautening. Her body ripened, strained as he readied her for his possession. The possession she yearned for, craved, was desperate for.

She heard her voice call his name, as if pleading with him. Pleading with him to complete what he had begun, to lift her to that plane of existence where fire and sweetness and unbearable light would fill her, where the rapture that only he could release in her would be.

He answered her, but she knew not what he said—knew only that his body was moving over hers, the strong, heavy weight of it as familiar as it had ever been, and her arms were snaking around him, enclosing him as her hips lifted to him, yearning for him, craving him, wanting only him, only this.

He thrust into her, a word breaking from him that she did not know but remembered well. The past and present fused, melded, became one. As if no years separated them. As if there had been no parting.

His possession filled her and her body enclosed his, embracing his even as her arms wrapped him to her. The strength of his lean, muscled form, the weight of it upon her, was crushing and yet arousing, even as his slow, rhythmic movements were arousing, and her legs wound about his as each thrust of his body pulsed the blood through her heated, straining body.

She wanted him—oh, dear God, how she wanted him—wanted this—wanted everything—everything he could give her.

He cried out—a straining roar—and as if it were a match to tinder she felt her body flood with him, with her, and she was lifted up, up, soaring into that other world that existed only at such times, forced through a barrier that was invisible, intangible in mortal life, but which now, in Anatole's arms, in his passion and embrace and the utter fusion of their bodies, was their sole existence. On and on she soared, crying into the wind as the heat of the sun in that other world burned down upon her.

Then, like the wind subsiding, she was drawn back down, panting, exhausted. *Sated.* Her whole body purged and cleansed in that white-hot air. She was shaking, trembling, and he was smoothing her hair, talking to her, withdrawing from her and yet folding her back against him, so that she was not alone, not bereft. She was crushed against him, his limbs enfolding hers, his arms wrapped tight around her, and his breath was warm on her shoulder, his hand curving around her cheek, his voice murmuring. She could feel the shuddering of his chest, the thudding of his heart that was in tune with hers.

He was saying her name, over and over again. The name he'd always called her. 'Tia, my Tia. *Mine.*'

And she *was* his. She was, and she always had been—she always would be. Always.

Sleep rushed over her, as impossible to resist as

if it had been slipped into her bloodstream like an overpowering drug. Her eyes fluttered closed. Muscles slackening, her body slumped into the protective cradle of his arms.

They tightened close around her.

CHAPTER TEN

MORNING WAS BREAKING over the gardens, reaching pale fingers of sun across the dew-drenched lawn. Christine stood at the window of her bedroom, a silk *peignoir* wrapping her, gazing blindly out. Her face was sombre, her thoughts far away into the past. The past that had become the present. The present she could not deny. Nor could she deny that she had allowed something to happen that should *never* have happened.

I called it insanity when he said we should marry. But what I've just done is insanity.

How could it be anything else? She turned her head, looking back towards the sleeping figure in her bed, the bedclothes carelessly stretched around his lean, golden-skinned body so that she could see the rise and fall of his chest—the chest she had clung to in that madness, that insanity of last night, as she had clung so often in that long-ago time that should have been *gone* for ever!

It has to be gone—it has to be! It's over!

And she could not, *must* not, allow it to be anything else. Whatever the unbearable temptation to do otherwise—a temptation that Anatole had made a million times more devastatingly powerful after what had happened last night.

I can't be what Anatole is telling me to be. Urging me to be. It's impossible—just impossible!

Impossible for so many reasons.

Impossible for just one overwhelming reason.

The same reason it's always been impossible.

Pain constricted her throat as she stared across at him now, where he lay sleeping in her bed.

There can be no future between us now—none. Just as there could be no future for us then.

She felt the breath tight in her lungs and moved to turn away. But as she did so she heard him stir, saw his hand reaching across the bed, his face registering her absence. His eyes sprang open and he saw her standing there. Emotion speared in his face but it was she who spoke first.

'You have to go! Right now! I can't have Mrs Hughes realising you spent the night here.'

His expression changed. 'But I did—and in your arms.'

He was defying her to deny it, his eyes holding hers. He sat up, reaching for her, catching her hand. Resting his hand on her flank, warm through the cool silk. Looking up at her.

'It's far too late for pretence,' he said softly. 'Didn't last night prove that to you?'

He drew her to him.

'Doesn't this prove it to you?'

His mouth lowered to hers. His kiss was like velvet—the kiss of a man who had taken possession of the woman he desired. She felt honey flow through her, felt her limbs tremble with it.

His eyes poured into hers, rich and lambent. 'It's happened, Tia.' His voice was as intimate, as hushed as if they were the only two people in the world. 'It's happened, and there's no going back now.'

She tried to pull away. Tried to free herself.

'There *has* to be!' she cried. 'I can't do what you want, Anatole. I can't—I *can't*!'

I mustn't! I daren't! What you are offering me is a temptation beyond my endurance. But I must endure it—I must.

She had endured it before—she must do so again. Must find refuge somehow. Find the strength to keep refusing him. Even now, after she had burned in his arms, in his embrace.

Now more than ever. Now that I know how weak I am...how helpless to resist you. Now that I know how hopelessly vulnerable I am to you. Now that I know the danger that stands before me.

Raggedly, she pulled free of him. 'I won't marry you, Anatole,' she said doggedly, each word tugged from her. 'I will not. Whatever you say to me—I will *not*.'

Who was she speaking to? Him or herself? She knew the answer. And she knew what that answer told her—knew the danger it proved her to be in.

Frustration flared in his eyes. 'Why? I don't understand? *Why*, Tia? How can you possibly deny what there is between us?'

She would not reply—could not. All she could do, with a desperate expression on her face, was beg him yet again to go. For an instant longer Anatole just stood there, then abruptly he stood up, seized up his discarded clothes, and disappeared into the en suite bathroom.

Rapidly, Christine got dressed too—pulling on a pair of jeans and a lightweight sweater, roughly brushing out the tangled hair that waved so wantonly around her shoulders, echoing her bee-stung lips in its sensuality...

With a smothered cry she whirled around to see Anatole emerge, wearing his clothes from the night before, but only the shirt and trousers. He looked... she gulped...he looked incredibly, devastatingly *sexy*. There was no other word for it—no other word to describe the slightly raffish look about him, compounded by the lock of raven hair falling across his forehead, the cuffs of his shirt pushed back casually, the dark shadow along his jawline.

She could not take her eyes from him—could feel her pulse quicken, the blood surging in her, colour flushing across her face, lips parting...

He saw her reaction and smiled. A slow, sensual smile, full of confidence.

'You see?'

It was all he said. All he needed to say. He walked towards her. *Strolled*.

She backed away, panic suddenly replacing her betraying reaction to his raw sexuality. 'No—Anatole, *no*! I won't let you do this to me—I *won't*!'

She held her hands up as if to ward him off. He halted, his expression changing. When he spoke there was frustration in his voice, and challenge, in equal measure.

'Tia, you cannot ignore what has happened.'

'I am *not* Tia! I am not her any more—and I will *never* be her again!'

The cry of her own voice, its vehemence, shocked

her. It seemed to shock Anatole as well. His eyes narrowed, losing that blatantly sexy half-lidded look with which he'd stared at her before. For a moment he did not speak. Just looked at her pale face, the cheekbones etched so starkly. Saw the tremble in her upheld hands.

'No,' he said quietly. 'You're not Tia. I've accepted that. I've accepted that you are Christine Kyrgiakis—Mrs Vasilis Kyrgiakis.'

The use of the description made her start. Made her hear the rest of what he said.

'The widow of my uncle—the mother of his son—the mother of my cousin.' He paused again, as if assessing her, the way she was reacting. 'I have made my case, *Christine*—' deliberately he used the name of the woman she was now, the woman she would always be going forward '—and I have given you the reasons why we should marry. And I believe I have done it in more than words.'

For a second that look was back in his eye—that heavy, half-lidded look that made her tremble as nothing that he could say could make her tremble, making her limbs turn boneless, her heart catch in mid-beat. Then he held up a hand, as if she had tried to interrupt him.

'But for now I'll leave it be. I understand, truly, that you must have time to get used to it. Time to come to terms with it. To see it as being as inevitable as I see it to be.' He took a breath, his tone changing. 'But for now the subject is closed. I accept that.'

He turned away, fetching his jacket, so carelessly thrown on a chair last night, and shrugging it on, tugging his cuffs clear and fastening them, then looking across at Christine again.

'I'll go now—to preserve the appearances that are, I know, so important to you right now.' There was no bite in his words, only acknowledgement. 'But I'll be back later. We have Nicky to collect—and, no, please don't tell me not to come with you. He'll be disappointed if I don't.'

She nodded in dumb acquiescence. It seemed easier than contesting his assertion. All she wanted—desperately—was for him to be out of here, finally to be able to collapse in a state of mental and emotional exhaustion, her body aching and spent.

She sheared her mind away—*no, don't think, not now. Not ever...*

But it was impossible not to think, not to feel, for the rest of the day, and when Anatole returned late in the afternoon—as he'd told her he would—so they could drive over to collect Nicky from the Barcourts, she felt a leap of unbearable emotion as her eyes went to his. And his to hers.

For a moment, as their eyes met, she felt as if she had been transported back in time and was poised to do what she had once done so automatically and spontaneously—run into his arms that would open to her and fold her to him.

Then his eyes were veiled and the moment passed. As he helped her into the car he made some pleasantry about the weather, to which she replied in kind. They chatted in a desultory way during the short journey, and Christine told herself she was thankful.

And she was even more thankful that as they arrived there was a melee to greet them: Elizabeth

Barcourt's grandchildren, their mother and their grandmother, all chattering to them madly.

As for Nicky—he was only too eager to regale them both with the delights of his day.

'I rode a pony! Can I have a pony—*can* I? Can I?' he pleaded, half to Anatole, half to Christine.

A spike drove into her heart as she saw the way her son addressed them both. As if he accepted her and Anatole as a unit. She tensed, and it was noticed by Elizabeth Barcourt, who drew her a little aside as Anatole crouched down to Nicky's level to get the full account of the joys of his day and the thrill of riding a pony for the first time.

'My dear, I'm glad Anatole is able to spend time with you—the more the better.' She cast a look at Christine, and then at Nicky. 'He's a natural with him! One might almost think—'

She broke off, as if conscious she had said too much, then stepped away, quietening her noisy grandchildren and telling them it was time for Nicky to head home.

As they finally set off Nicky's chatter was all of ponies and puppies and the fun he'd had with the other children.

'I'm going to paint a picture of a pony and a puppy,' he announced as they arrived, and then belied his intention by giving a huge yawn, indicating how little actual sleep his exciting sleepover had involved.

'Bath first,' said Christine, and then hesitated.

What she wanted to do was tell Anatole it was time for him to leave, to go away, to leave her alone with her son. But her hesitation was fatal.

'Definitely bath time,' Anatole said, adding with a grin, 'I'll race you upstairs!'

With a cry of excitement Nicky set off up the wide staircase and Anatole followed—as did Christine, much more slowly, her face set.

OK, so the two of them would bath Nicky, and see him to bed and *then* she'd tell Anatole it was time he left. That was her intention—her absolute resolve. Because no way was he going to spend the night here again.

And not in my bed!

Her face flushed with colour, her features contorting.

He's got to go—he's just got to.

Close to an hour later, with Nicky tucked up in bed and falling asleep instantly, she walked back downstairs with Anatole. She paused at the foot and turned to him.

'Are you staying at the White Hart tonight or heading straight back to London?' Her voice was doggedly bright, refusing to acknowledge there was any other possibility.

He looked at her. His gaze was half lidded, as if he knew why she was saying what she was.

'Once,' he said, 'you were not so rejecting of me.'

The expression in his eyes, the open caress in his voice, brought colour to stain her cheekbones, and her fingers clenched at her sides.

'Once,' she replied, 'I was a different person.'

He gave a swift shake of his head, negating her denial. 'You're still that person—whether you call yourself Tia or Christine, you're still her. And last night showed me that. It showed *you* that! So why deny it?

Why even *try* to deny it? Why try to deny that our marriage would work?'

And now the caress was back in his voice, almost tangible on her skin, which was suddenly flushing with heat.

'Last night showed how alive that flame that was always between us still is. From the moment you saw me, Tia, you wanted me—and I wanted you. I wanted you then and I want you now. And it is the same for you. It blazes from you, your desire for me.'

He reached a hand towards her, long lashes sweeping down over his eyes, a half-smile pulling at his mouth.

'Don't deny it, Tia,' he said softly. 'Don't deny the truth of what we have. We *burn* for each other.' His voice dropped to a sensual husk.

She took a jerky step backwards—an instinctive gesture of self-protection against what he wanted. He didn't like it that she did so, and he stilled. She lifted her chin. Looked straight at him. She must tell him what she needed to say. What he needed to hear.

Her eyes met his unflinchingly, with a bare, stark expression in them. 'I know that, Anatole! Dear God, of *course* I know it! How could I not?'

She shook her head, as if acknowledging a truth she could not deny. Then her eyes reached his, hung on to his, trying to make him hear, understand.

'It was always like that—right from the first. And, yes, it's still there. Last night did prove it, just as you say. But, Anatole, listen—*listen* to me. I can't let myself be blinded by passion! And nor can you! A marriage can't be built on passion alone, and nor can it be based on just wanting to make a family for Nicky. You *have* to see that!'

There was a tremor in her voice, intensity in her face—but in his there was only blank rejection of her rejection of him.

'All my life,' he said slowly, 'women have wanted to marry me. You included, or so I supposed way back then. And yet now, when I *want* to marry, the woman I want to marry is turning me down.' He gave a laugh. There was no humour in it. 'Maybe that's some kind of cosmic karma—I don't know.'

He pressed his lips together, as if to control his words, his emotions. Emotions that were streaming through him in a way he had never known before. A kind of disbelief. Even dismay.

His eyes rested on her. 'So, what *can* a marriage be built on? Tell me what else there needs to be.'

She looked at him, and there was a deep sadness in her voice as she answered. 'Oh, Anatole, the fact that you have to ask tells me how impossible marriage would be between us.'

'Then *tell* me!' he ground out.

She shut her eyes for a moment, shaking her head before she opened them again. She looked at him, her features twisting. 'I can't,' she said. 'But...' She paused, as if profoundly reluctant to speak, yet she did so. 'You would know it—'

She broke off, turned away, walked unevenly towards the front door to open it for him to leave. Marriage between them was as impossible now as it had been when she'd thought she lived in fairyland.

Emotion was pressing upon her—unbearable, agonising—but she would not yield to it. Opening the door, she turned back to him. He hadn't moved. He was just looking at her.

Determinedly, she met his gaze. 'Anatole—please—' She indicated the open doorway.

He walked towards it, pausing beside her. 'We'd make a good couple,' he said. 'We'd have each other and Nicky. Maybe a child of our own one day.'

A smothered cry came from her. '*Go!* Go, Anatole, and leave me alone!'

She closed the door on him, not caring that she'd all but pushed him out. Only when the lock clicked, cutting out the sound of his footsteps on the gravelled drive, muffling the sound of his car door slamming, the engine starting, did she turn, leaning back on the closed front door, shutting him out—out of her house, out of her life.

A child of our own...

That muffled cry came again. That was what she had longed for so long ago—before the glowing fairy dust she'd sprinkled over her life had turned to bitter ashes.

Slowly, bleakly, she headed upstairs to kiss her sleeping son a silent goodnight.

The only person she could love.

Could allow herself to love.

CHAPTER ELEVEN

'MY DEAR, IT'S good to see you again. How are you bearing up?'

It was the vicar's wife, welcoming her into the vicarage where her husband offered her a dry sherry.

'I miss my weekly symposia with Vasilis,' he said, after his wife had asked after Nicky, and how he too was bearing up.

This kind of kind enquiry had continued to come her way, and Christine always answered as best she could. But it was difficult. How could she possibly tell people that Anatole had offered her marriage in order to make a family for Nicky? An offer she could not accept, however overwhelming the temptation.

That temptation still wound itself inside her head even now—despite all she felt, all she told herself, all she had forced herself to feel, not to feel, in the endless month that had passed since Anatole had driven away that last time.

It had been a month filled with anguish and torment over what she had done. A month of missing Anatole.

And that was the worst of it—the most dangerous sign of all—telling her what she so desperately did not want to be told. She longed to be able to put him out

of her mind, but it was impossible. And made more
so by Nicky's repeated mentions of him, his constant
questioning about when Anatole would be back.

'I want him to come!' he would say plaintively, and
Christine and Nanny Ruth would be hard pressed to
divert him, even though summer was coming and the
weather warm enough for them to think of driving to
the coast, for a day at the beach.

'But I want Cousin Anatole to come too!' had been
Nicky's only response when she'd told him. 'Why can't
he come? *Why?*'

Christine had done her best. 'Munchkin, your
cousin works very hard—he has lots to do. He has to
fly to other countries—'

'He could fly *here*,' Nicky had retaliated. He'd
looked across at his mother. 'He could *live* here. He
said he was coming to look after me—he *said*. He said
my *pappou* told him to!'

His little face had quivered, and Christine's heart
had gone out to him. Pangs had pierced her.

If she married Anatole—

No! It was madness to think of yielding. Worse
than madness. It would be sentencing herself to a lifetime of anguish.

Instead she had to sentence her beloved son to missing Anatole.

When the first postcard had arrived, she'd been
grateful. It had been from Paris, showing the Eiffel
Tower and a popular cartoon character. Anatole had
written on the back.

*Will you do me a painting of the Eiffel Tower,
with you and me at the top?*

Nicky, thrilled, had rushed off to get his paints.

More postcards had arrived, one every week, from different parts of the globe. And now a month had turned into six weeks. Six endless weeks.

The imminent arrival of his puppy was a source of cheer, and learning to ride, being taught as promised by Giles, helped keep Nicky busy—as did the open day at the pre-prep school he would start at in the autumn.

After meeting some of the other boys there who would be his classmates Christine had arranged some play dates. She'd even thought about taking Nicky away on holiday for a week somewhere. Perhaps a theme park. Perhaps the seaside in Brittany or Spain.

She didn't know. Couldn't decide. Couldn't think. Couldn't do anything except let one day slip by into another and feel a kind of quiet, drear despair seep over her.

Was this to be her life from now on? It seemed so lonely without Anatole.

I miss him!

The cry came from deep within, piercing in its intensity. She tried to think of Vasilis, to use his calm, comforting memory to insulate herself—but Vasilis was fading. His presence in the house, her life, was only a fragile echo.

She felt him most when she attended to the business of his foundation, but that was intermittent, with the meat of the work being carried out by his hand-picked trustees, who followed the programme her husband had set out for them. She did her bit, played her part, had gone twice to London for meetings, but on her return there was only one man she thought about.

Only one.

The one she could not have.

The one she had sent away.

And the one whom she missed more and more with every passing day.

Anatole was back in Athens again. He'd spent weeks flying from one city to another, relentlessly restless, driven onwards by frustration and a punishing need to keep occupied and keep moving, putting out of his mind all that he had left behind.

The only times he let it intrude was when he paused in airports to buy a postcard for Nicky of wherever he happened to be, scrawling something on it for the boy.

But it did not do to think too much of Nicky. Still less of Christine. Instead, he made himself focus on what had landed on him here in Athens.

His face set in a grim expression. Both parents had demanded that he visit, and both visits had been hideous. His father intended to get yet another divorce, and wanted a way of getting out of the pre-nup he'd so rashly signed, and his mother wanted him to get back a villa on the Italian lakes she regretted allowing her most recent ex to have.

He was interested in neither demand, nor in the flurry of social invitations that had descended upon him to functions at which women would make a bee-line for him, as they always did, his unmarried status a honeypot to them. It had always been like that and he was fed up with it—more fed up than he'd ever been in his life.

I don't want any of this. I don't want to be here. I don't want these people in my life.

Neither the women fawning over him, trying to get his interest, nor his parasitic parents, who only contacted him when they wanted something from him and otherwise ignored his existence, were anything other than repellent to him. And as he headed back to his apartment—alone—he knew with a kind of fierceness that ran like fire in his veins that in all the six punishing weeks he'd spent travelling the world there had been only one place he wanted to get back to. Only one place he wanted to be.

He walked out on to his balcony and the heat of the city's night seemed suffocating. Clogging his lungs. Memory sliced through him, pushing a different balcony high up in the London rooftops into his mental vision. A greenish glow lit the greenery…a soft voice exclaimed at the sight.

A soft voice that had cried out to him again after so many years as they had reached ecstasy together once more. Before that same voice, soft no longer, had banished him.

A vice seemed to close around him, crushing him. He had lost her once before, through his own blindness. Now he had lost her again and he could not endure it.

I have to see her again. I have to try again—I can't give up on her. I want a family—a family with her, with Nicky.

And why should she not want that too? What impediment could there be?

Across his mind, her words drifted like a ghost intent on haunting him.

'You would know it—'

What had she meant? What did she want that he

was not offering her? What was necessary to a good marriage other than what he had set out in plain words, in every caress that he had lavished upon her?

It made no sense.

He shook the thoughts from him, impatient to be gone, to close the yawning space between where he was and where she and Nicky were.

Within hours, those parting miles had vanished, and as he sped out of Heathrow, heading south, gaining open countryside, for the first time since he had left he felt his spirits lighten, his breathing ease.

Elation filled him. And hope renewed. This time— surely this time—he would persuade Christine to finally make her future with him.

This time she won't refuse me.

Hope, strong and powerful, streamed within him.

Christine turned in between the wrought-iron gates, the wheels of her car crunching over the gravel. She'd just collected Nicky from another riding lesson at the Barcourts', and now he was imparting Giles's equine wisdom to his mother.

'You mustn't let ponies eat too much grass,' he informed her. 'It blows them up like a balloon. They might pop!'

'Oh, dear,' said Christine dutifully.

'And you have to groom them after *every* ride. I groom Bramble—but not his tail. Giles does that. Ponies can kick if they get cross.'

'Oh, dear,' Christine said again, thankful that Giles had performed that tricky office.

'I did his mane. I stood on a box to reach,' continued Nicky. 'Bramble is a strawberry roan. He's thirteen hands. That means how high he is. When I'm grown up I'll be too big for him. Now I'm almost just right.'

Murmuring appropriately, Christine rounded the bend in the drive, emerging from the shade into the sunshine that was bathing the gracious frontage of the house, with its pleasing symmetry and the dormer windows in the roofline. The sunshine that was gleaming off the silver-grey saloon car just drawing up ahead of her.

She felt her stomach clench. Her pulse leap. Her breath catch. Anatole was emerging from the car, looking round as he heard her approach, lifting a hand in greeting.

Nicky stopped in mid-word and cried out, ecstatic delight and excitement in his voice, 'He came—he *came*! I wanted him to and he has!'

The next few minutes passed in a blur as, trying urgently to quell the tumult inside her, Christine drew her car up beside Anatole's. Nicky, overjoyed, scrambled out to hurl himself at Anatole, who scooped him in a single sweep up into his arms, clutching him tightly.

Exhilaration streamed through Anatole at the feel of the little lad embracing him. It was good, *so* good to see him again—more than good. Wonderful!

'Oof!' he exclaimed laughingly. 'You're getting heavier and heavier, young man!'

He ruffled the dark hair—as dark as his own, thought Christine, and felt the familiar ache shooting inside her—then lowered Nicky to the ground. He looked across at Christine.

'Hi,' he said casually. Determinedly casually. Determinedly suppressing the urge, the overpowering desire to do to her as he'd done to Nicky—sweep her up into his arms and hug her tightly! But he must not do that. He must be calm, casual. Friendly, nothing but friendly.

For now.

His expression changed slightly. 'Sorry to drop in unannounced. I hope it's OK.' He paused, then said deliberately, 'I'm booked in at the White Hart.'

He wanted to give her no excuse for sending him away again. To do nothing to scare her off.

Wordlessly, she nodded, feeling relief for that, at least. She was trying to get her composure back, but it was impossible. Impossible to do anything but feel the rapid surge of her blood, the hectic flare of colour in her cheeks as her eyes hung on him.

He was in casual clothes—designer jeans and a sweater with a designer logo on it, and designer sneakers. He looked totally relaxed and like a million dollars. She felt her heart start to thump.

'I'd better let Mrs Hughes know you'll be here for dinner,' she said, finally managing to speak.

He tilted an eyebrow at her. 'Not if you have other plans.'

She had no plans—nothing except helping Nanny Ruth with Nicky's tea, bath time and bed. Then her own TV supper in her sitting room.

She made herself smile. 'I'm sure Nicky will want to eat with you.'

'Yes! *Yes!*' Her son tugged at Anatole's jeans. 'Come and play with me. I've been for a ride. And I groomed Bramble. Giles says I'm going to be jumping him soon!'

'Are you, now?' Anatole grinned, letting himself focus on the lad.

He didn't look again at Christine. It would not have been wise.

She was looking...*beautiful*—that was what she was looking. Beautiful, with her hair pushed off her face by a band, wearing a summery skirt in a blue-printed material, gathered at the waist, and a pale yellow blouse with a short cardigan in a deeper yellow. Her legs were bare, showing golden calves, and her narrow feet were in espadrilles.

He felt desire leap instantly within him. And an emotion that he could not name kicked through him, powerful and unfamiliar. He wanted to go on looking at her. More than look. Wanted to close the distance between them, take her face in his hands and kiss her sweet, tender mouth—as a husband would a wife.

Determination swept through him. *I have to make her mine. I have to persuade her, convince her how right it is for us to marry! Overcome her objections...*

Into his head came her words again—the words he could not understand but needed to understand, about just what it was that she was holding out for.

'You would know it—'

Frustration ground at him again. *What* would he know? What was it she wanted of him that he was not offering her?

I have to find out.

And that was why he had come, wasn't it? To try again—and again.

I'll never give up—never!

The knowledge seared in him, infusing every brain cell with its power. But then Nicky was tugging at

him again, chattering away, reclaiming his attention—
which he gave with a leap of his emotion to see the
boy so eager to be with him. He grinned down fondly
at him, and let Nicky drag him off.

Christine watched them go indoors, feeling as if
a sledgehammer had just swiped her sideways. Jerk-
ily, she put her car away in the garage, went indoors
via the kitchen to seek out Mrs Hughes about revis-
ing dinner plans, then she hurried to the sanctuary of
her bedroom, her heart hammering, her emotions in
tumultuous free fall.

She knew she couldn't keep Anatole out of Nicky's
life indefinitely, but how could she possibly bear to
keep on seeing him turn up like this…turning her up-
side down and inside out all over again?

Of their own volition her eyes went to her bed—
the bed where she had made love with Anatole in that
insane yielding to her own impossible desire for him.

Biting her lip, as if to bite off a memory she must
not allow, she headed for her bathroom.

Her cheeks were far too hot. And there was only
one cause of that…

As Mrs Hughes wheeled in dinner, it was like *déjà
vu* for Christine, as she remembered that first time—
so long ago now, it seemed—when Anatole had invited himself.

Nicky, in fine fettle and fresh from bath time, in py-
jamas and dressing gown, was exclaiming to Anatole
that it would be pasta for dinner. Anatole was saying
it would liver and spinach.

'No! No!' cried Nicky, unconvinced. 'That's for
you!' He gave a peal of laughter.

'Yummy!' retorted Anatole, rubbing his midriff. 'My favourite!'

'Yucky-yuck-yuck!' Nicky rejoined, repeating it for good measure, with another peal of laughter.

Christine calmed him down—getting him over-excited was not sensible. But then, dining here with her son and Anatole was not sensible either, was it? It was the very opposite of sensible. It was little short of criminally stupid.

But how could she deprive her son of what he was clearly enjoying so much? Emotion slid under skin. If she succumbed to Anatole's proposal, this might be their way of life...

For a moment she saw the glitter of fairy dust over the scene. She and Anatole, Nicky with them, day after day, night after night. A family. A fairytale come true.

Into her head she heard the words that Elizabeth Barcourt had spoken. *'He's a natural with him!'* And the half-sentence that had followed. *'Almost as if—'*

No! The guillotine sliced down again and she bus-ied herself helping Mrs Hughes.

In yet another replay of that first time Anatole had dined here, the housekeeper proffered wine for Ana-tole's inspection—and this time it did not grate with her, Anatole taking his uncle's role.

Vasilis seemed so very far away now—and she found it hurt her to realise just how long ago their marriage seemed. As if she were leaving him behind.

'You're thinking of my uncle, aren't you?'

Anatole's voice was quiet and his eyes were on her, Christine realised, as Mrs Hughes left the room.

She nodded, blinking. Then she felt a gentle pres-sure on her arm. Anatole had leant across to press his hand softly on her sleeve. The gesture was simple, and yet it made Christine stare at him, confusion in her gaze. There was something in his eyes she'd never seen before. Something that made her throat tighten.

For a moment their eyes held.

'Mumma, *please* may I start?' Nicky's voice broke the moment.

'Yes—but say Grace first,' said Christine with a smile at her son. A smile that somehow flickered to Anatole as well, and was met with an answering flicker.

In his sing-song voice Nicky recited Grace, with an angelic expression on his face and his hands pressed together in dutiful reverence, rounding off with Giles Barcourt's reminder that puddings came to those who were good.

Anatole laughed and they all tucked in—Nicky to his beloved pasta, Christine and Anatole to a delicious chicken fricassee. As she sipped her wine she felt the difference in atmosphere at this meal from the meal when Anatole had first descended on them.

How much easier it was now.

How much more natural it seemed.

As if it's right for him to be here.

She felt the pull of it like a powerful tide, drawing ever closer. A dangerous tide of overwhelming temptation. But if she indulged—

She tore her mind away, focussing on the moment, on Nicky's chatter, on Anatole's easy replies and her own deliberately neutral contributions when necessary.

As the meal ended, with pudding consumed, Nicky started to yawn copiously. Between them, she and

Anatole carried him up to bed, saw him off to sleep, then slowly headed downstairs.

The Greek words of the night-time blessing Anatole had once again murmured over the sleeping child, resonated in Christine's head. And, as if it did in his too, Anatole spoke.

'What arrangements are being made to ensure that Nicky grows up bilingual? I'm sure Vasilis would have wanted that. Obviously I'll do my best, but if I only visit occasionally he may well lose what he has already.'

There was no criticism in his voice, only enquiry.

Christine nodded, acknowledging his reasonable concern. 'Yes, something must be arranged.' She gave a slight smile. 'Our vicar promised Vasilis that he'd teach Nicky classical Greek in a few years, but that won't be enough, I know. I can manage a little modern Greek—enough to teach him the alphabet, but nothing more. Maybe…' she glanced cautiously at Anatole '…maybe you could chat to him regularly over the Internet? And ensure he has contemporary Greek language children's literature to read?'

She started to walk downstairs again. It was not unreasonable to encourage Nicky to keep up his Greek with Anatole—surely it wasn't?

I have to learn to live in harmony with Anatole. Whatever happens, I can't refuse him that.

Her mind skittered away, not wanting to think about the rest of her life with Anatole interacting with Nicky over the years. It was too difficult.

Instead, she went on, 'I could have a word with his headmaster—see if he can recommend a tutor in modern Greek when he starts school in September?'

'School?' Anatole frowned.

'Yes—Vasilis enrolled him at the nearby pre-prep school. It's the same one Giles Barcourt went to. Very traditional, but very well regarded. We both liked it when we visited—and so did Nicky. He's looking forward to starting.'

'Is it a boarding school?' There was a harsh note in Anatole's sharp question.

Christine stared at him. 'Of course it isn't! I wouldn't *dream* of sending him to boarding school! If he actually *wants* to board, when he's a teenager, then fine—but obviously not till then...if at all.'

She saw Anatole's face relax. 'My apologies. It's just that—' He broke off, then resumed as his heavy tread headed downstairs ahead of her. 'I was packed off to boarding school when I was seven. I was a nuisance to my parents, and they wanted shot of me.'

There was harshness in his voice. More than harshness. *Pain.*

She caught up with him as he reached the hall, grabbed his arm. 'Oh, Anatole, that's awful! How could they *bear* to?' There was open shock and sympathy in her voice.

A hollow laugh was her answer. 'I wasn't a priority for them—'

He broke off again, and into Christine's head came a memory from five years ago, when she'd told him how much she missed her father, and he'd told her she was lucky to have any good memories of him at all.

'In a way,' he said, and there was a twist in his voice that was very audible to her, 'Vasilis cared more for me in his abstract manner than either of my parents did. Maybe,' he went on, not looking at her, but look-

ing inwardly, 'that's why I so want Nicky to have me
in his life. So I can be to Vasilis's son what he was to
me. But…more so.'

His eyes went to her, and there was a veiled expression in them.

'I want you both, Christine. You *and* Nicky. That
will not change.'

His eyes held hers, and what she saw in them told
her why he had come here.

She made herself hold his gaze. Made herself
speak to him. 'And nor will my answer, Anatole.'
Her voice was steady, though she felt her emotions
bucking wildly inside her. But she must hold steady.
She *must*.

Frustration flashed across his features. '*Why?* It
makes such *sense* for us to marry!'

Her throat was tight, and her hands were clasping
each other as she faced him. 'It made sense for me
to marry Vasilis. At least…' she took a painful breath
'…it seemed to at the time.' Her eyes were strained,
her cheekbones etched. 'I won't—' She swallowed,
feeling the tightness in her throat. 'I won't marry again
for the same reason.'

*And not you, Anatole! Not you over whom I once
sprinkled fairy dust only to have it turn to ashes.*

She lifted up her hands in that warding off gesture
she had made last time. It made him want to step towards her, deny her negation of him. Frustration bit
in him, and more than frustration. A stronger emotion
he could not name.

But she was speaking again, not letting him coun-
ter her, try to argue her down, make her accept what
he could see so clearly.

'Anatole, *please*!' There was strain in her voice now, and her face was working. 'Please. I cannot—*will* not—marry you to make a family for Nicky!' She gave a weary sigh. 'Oh, Anatole, we're going round in circles. I don't want what *you* want.'

'Then what *do* you want?' he cried out, with a frustration that shook him in its intensity.

Yet even as he spoke he heard her words, spoken to him the last time they'd stood here, going round in the circles they were caught in, round and round, repeating the impasse of their opposition.

You would know it—

The words mocked him, taunted him. He wanted to knock them to the floor, get them out of the way, because they came between him and what he wanted so much—to crush her to him and smother her with kisses, to sweep her up the stairs and into her room, her bed. To make her his own for ever!

But he did not. For yet again they were caught in that endless loop they were trapped in, and she was doing what he had seen her do before.

He saw her walk to the door, open it, to usher him out—out of her life again. As she always did. Always had from the very moment she had left him to marry his uncle.

On heavy tread he did as she bid him, feeling as though gravity were crushing him.

'May I visit tomorrow?' The words sounded abrupt, though he did not mean them to be.

She nodded. Nicky would expect it. Long for it. How could she deprive her son of what gave him such delight?

How can I deprive him of what Anatole is offering?

Like a serpent in her veins, temptation coiled in its dangerous allure. Tightening its fatal grip on her.

'Thank you,' Anatole said quietly.

He paused, looked at her in the doorway. Behind her in the hall he could hear the grandfather clock ticking steadily, measuring out their lives. Their *separate* lives. The thought was anguish to him.

Then he made himself give her a flickering smile, bid her goodnight. He walked out into the summer's night, heard an owl calling from the woodlands, smelled the scent of honeysuckle wafting at him.

From the doorway she watched him go...watched the car drive off, its headlights sweeping through the dark, cutting a path of light. And then he was gone. Gone yet again.

Was this what her life was to be now? Anatole arriving and departing? Spending time with her only to see Nicky, watching him grow up as year followed year? How could she bear it?

In the quiet hallway she heard the clock ticking past the seconds, the months, the years ahead.

A sudden smothered cry broke from her and she turned away, heading back indoors, shutting the door.

Alone once more.

So alone.

CHAPTER TWELVE

ANATOLE STOOD BY the open window in his bedroom, looking out over the walled garden of the White Hart. Dawn was stealing in, heralding the new day. But not new hope.

His expression was sombre and drawn. His journey here had been in vain. It was pointless to have made it. She had refused him again. Had told him she would always refuse him.

She does not want me.

That was what it came down to. Her rejection of him. She had rejected him when she'd left him to marry Vasilis. She was rejecting him still.

A bitter twist contorted his lips as he stood staring bleakly. He should be used to rejection. Should have got used to it from a young age. He had been rejected by his own parents—who had never wanted him, never loved him.

His mind sheared away from ancient pain. Why was he thinking about that now? He'd always known he wasn't important to them. Had learnt to insulate himself from it. Learnt to ignore it. Discard it. Do without it. He had always lived his life without love. Without wanting love.

He frowned. Why waste his thoughts on his parents? They were not important to him. It was Tia who was important. Tia and her son Nicky.

His expression softened, the twist of his lips relaxing, curving into a fond, reminiscent smile that lit up his eyes as he recalled how wonderful it had been to be greeted by his young cousin so eagerly, to spend the evening with him, absorbed in his world. As Nicky had hurtled towards him, and as he'd caught him up into his arms, an emotion so fierce had swept him, rushing through him like a freight train. Overwhelming him.

What was it, that emotion that had possessed him? A joy so intense, a lifting of his heart that he felt again now, even in recalling it? What *was* that emotion? He'd felt nothing like it before—never in his life.

And it had stayed with him, intensified, curving right through him as his eyes had gone to Christine— so beautiful, so lovely, and so very dear to him.

How can I live without her? Without them both?

He couldn't. It was impossible.

I can't live without them. I need them to breathe, to keep my heart beating!

His expression changed as he rested his gaze on the deep-shadowed garden.

Why? *Why* did he need them to breathe, to keep his heart beating? *Why* did that fierce, protective emotion possess him when he hefted Nicky into his arms? When he gazed at Christine? What *was* it that he felt with such burning intensity?

On the far side of the garden, towards the east, the sky was lightening, tipping the outlines of the ornamental trees and the edges of their silhouetted branches with light. He stood staring at them, feeling inside that same emotion building again, filling him, confusing him, bewildering him.

He heard his own voice calling silently inside his head.

Tia, tell me! Tell me what it is I feel about you. About Nicky.

And in his head he heard her, answering him with the words she'd said that had so confused him, bewildered him.

'*You would know it—*'

He heard the words that completed what she'd said. What she had not said.

If you felt it.

Slowly, oh-so-slowly, as if the whole world had turned about, the two phrases came together—fused.

You would know it if you felt it.

And suddenly, out of nowhere—out of an absence in his being that had been there all his life—he was filled: filled with a rush, a flood of realisation. Of understanding, of knowledge.

That was why he needed her to keep his heart beating! That was why he needed her to breathe!

That was the emotion that he felt—the emotion he knew because he felt it.

It was an emotion he had never known in his life, for no one had ever felt it about *him*—no one had ever taught him how to recognise it.

Accept it.

Feel it.

That was the emotion he felt when he thought about Christine, about Nicky. *That* was what had brought him here to be with them, to beg her to let him stay

with her and Nicky all his life. To make a family together.

That was the emotion that filled him now—filled
him in every cell in his body—the emotion that was
turning his heart over and over and over as realisation
poured through him.

He stood there breathless with it, stunned with it.
Stood stock-still as he gazed out into the garden which
was filling now with gold…with the risen sun.

As he stood there, with the world turning to gold
around him, turning to gold within him, he knew
there was only one thing to be done right now. To
find Christine and tell her.

'You would know it—' she had told him.

Triumph and gratitude, wonder and thankfulness
seared him. Well, now he knew—and it was time to
tell her. Oh, time to tell her indeed!

Pulling away from the window, he hurried to dress.

Christine was having breakfast on the little stone-
paved terrace beyond her sitting room, with Nicky
seated opposite her. Nanny Ruth was upstairs, packing
for her weekend away to visit her sister. The morning
was warm already, the garden filled with sunshine and
birdsong, rich with the scent and colour of flowers.

Nicky was chattering away, talking to her about
what they would do when Anatole arrived. 'Can we
go to the holiday park again? Can we? Can we?' he
asked eagerly.

'I don't know, munchkin—let's wait and see,' she
temporised.

Her mood was torn. Hammered down under a barrier as impenetrable as she could make it, battering to

be let out, was an emotion she must not feel. The raw, overpowering eagerness to see Anatole again, to let her eyes light upon him, drink him in. But she must not let that emotion break through. If it did—

I might crack, and yield. Give in to what I so long to do, which would bring me nothing but misery and anguish.

No, all she could do was what she was trying so hard to do now—crush down that desperately dangerous longing, suppress it tightly, keep it leashed so that it never broke through.

I've got to be careful! Oh, so careful!

She had to learn how to school herself, how to manage what would from now on be the routine of her life. She had to learn to face seeing Anatole on and off, whenever he visited Nicky through all the years ahead—years that stretched like a torment before her. Wanting so much…yearning for what she could not have. What she had always yearned for but had never had.

She reached for her coffee as Nicky munched his toast, still happily chattering. Lifted her cup to her mouth to take a sip. And stilled in mid-lift.

Anatole was striding across the gardens towards her.

He'd come from the direction of the boundary wall, and the woodland beyond, and a dim part of her mind wondered why. But the rest of her consciousness was leaping into ultra-focus, her gaze fastening on him, that emotion leaping within her that she must not feel but could not suppress as he drew closer. Her clinging gaze took in his ruffled hair, the soft leather jacket he was wearing over a dark blue sweater, his long, lithe jeans-clad legs covering the dew damp lawn in seconds.

He came up to them. Nicky, sitting with his back to him, hadn't noticed him.

Anatole's eyes went to her in a sudden, flickering gaze that was only brief, but she felt a tingle of shock go through her. In it had been something she had never seen before—but an instant later it had gone...gone before she could even wonder at it. She only know that as his gaze flicked away she felt a sense of empty desolation in her so strong she almost sobbed.

Then a grin was slicing his face, and his hands were sliding around Nicky's eyes. 'Guess who?' he said.

Nicky squealed in delight, grabbing Anatole's hands and clambering down to rush around the chair to hug his legs and greet him deliriously.

Then he pulled away sharply. 'You're all wet!' he said indignantly.

Anatole hunkered down beside him to hug him. His heart was pounding, and not just from the long walk he'd had. 'I came on foot,' he said, 'and there's a lot of long damp grass in those fields!'

Christine stared weakly. 'But it's five miles!' she exclaimed.

He only shrugged, for a second making that flickering eye contact with her again that left her reeling and then desolate when he broke it, and laughed.

'It's a glorious morning—it was a joy to walk!' He pulled out one of the ironwork chairs at the table and sat himself down. 'I could murder a coffee,' he said.

Like an echo, piercing and sibilant, memory stabbed into Christine. He'd used those same words five long years ago, when he'd taken her to his London apartment.

Numbly, she got to her feet. 'I'll... I'll go and make some fresh,' she said, her emotions in turmoil at his unexpectedly early arrival.

In the kitchen, she tried to calm herself. What use was it for her heart to leap the way it did when she set eyes on him? What use at all? What use to feel that dreadful, desolate ache inside her?

Forcibly, she took deep breaths, and when she went back out with a fresh cafetière of coffee, plus toast and some warmed croissants, she felt a little less agitated.

But it only took the sight of Anatole sitting with Nicky at the table, laughing and smiling, to make her feel weak again, to know how useless her attempts to cope with this would be.

'We're going to the beach! We're going to the beach!'

Her son's excited piping made her turn her attention to him.

'Beach?' she echoed vaguely, her mind still churning.

'We can make a day of it.' Anatole grinned. Then his expression changed. 'If that's acceptable to you?'

She nodded. Now that the magic word 'beach' had been uttered it would be impossible to withdraw it without tears from Nicky.

'I'll need to get our beach things packed up,' she said.

Getting away from him again would give her respite, allow her to steady her nerves, arm herself against his presence.

But his arm reached out. 'Don't rush off,' he said.

He took a breath. Met her eyes. That same strange, unreadable flicker was in them that had caught at her so powerfully. She felt herself tense. Something had changed about him, but she didn't know what.

Then he was turning to Nicky. 'Why don't you run upstairs and tell Nanny Ruth we're going to go to the beach?' he said, making his voice encouraging.

Excited, Nicky hared off.

Anatole turned back to Christine. For a second— less than a second—there was complete silence. It seemed to fill the space, the world between them. Then he spoke.

'I need to talk to you,' he said.

There was an intensity in his voice, in his expression, that stilled her completely.

'What is it?' she asked, alarm in her words.

There was something in his eyes that was making her heart suddenly beat faster—something she'd seen in that brief second when he'd arrived.

'Can we walk across the garden?' he asked.

Numbly, she nodded, and Anatole fell into place beside her.

An intense nervous energy filled him. So much depended on the next few minutes.

Everything depends on it—my whole life—

'Anatole, what's wrong?'

Christine's voice penetrated his hectic thoughts. There was a thread of anxiety audible in her tone.

He didn't answer until they'd crossed the lawn into a little dell of beech trees dappled with sunlight, where there was a rustic wooden bench. She sat down, and so did he, wanting to take her hand, but not daring to. His heart was slugging in his chest.

Christine's eyes were on him, wide with alarm. 'Anatole...' she said again, faintly.

Something was wrong—the same dread that had assailed her that nightmare morning when she'd had to tell him she thought she was pregnant was rising up to bite in her lungs.

'Christine...' He took a breath, a ragged one, wanting to look at her, but not wanting to, instead fixing his gaze on the beech mast littering the ground. 'Last night...' He paused, then forced himself on. 'Last night you said you would never marry me just because it made sense to do so, just to make a family for Nicky. And the time before—that morning after,' he said, daring, finally, to steal a glance at her, seeing in a brief instant how still her face was, how taut with tension—how beautiful.

Emotion sliced through him, but he had to blank it. Had to get the words out he needed to say.

'You said you would never marry me just because... because of how good we are together.'

He did not spell it out further—the flush in her cheeks showed him he did not need to.

'You told me...' He drew another breath, 'You told me that there was only one reason you would marry again. And that I would know it...'

He paused again, hearing birdsong in the trees, rustling in the undergrowth. The sounds of life were going on all around him and the world was stretching from here to eternity, all in absolute focus—while he was putting to the test the single thing that would mean everything to him for the rest of his life.

'I know it,' he said quietly.

At his side he felt her still—still completely, as if her very breathing had ceased.

'I know it,' he said again.

And now his eyes went to her, his head turning. Her face was a mask, the pallor in it draining all the blood from her skin. Her eyes were huge. Distended in her face. And in them was something he had never seen revealed before. He felt it like a sudden stabbing of his heart.

But it was there, and he knew it for the very first time in his life—because for the very first time in his life it was in his own eyes, in his face, in his very being as well.

'It's love, isn't it, Tia?' He said her old name without conscious thought, only with emotion. An emotion he had never felt before, never recognised, never believed in.

Until now.

'Love,' he said again. 'That's what you said we needed. The only reason to marry.'

He lifted a single finger to her cheek, felt the soft silk of its texture.

'Love,' he said again.

It was strange…the tip of his finger was wet, and he lifted it away. There was the faintest runnel of moisture on her cheek, below her eye. Another came from the other side. He saw her blink, saw another diamond catch the light and spill softly, quietly.

'Tia!' His voice was filled with alarm. 'Oh, Tia—I don't mean to make you weep!'

But it was too late. Far too late. A cry broke from her—a cry that had been five long years in its engendering. A cry that broke the deadly, anguished turmoil of her heart.

His arms swept around her, hugging her to him,

holding her close until she wept no more. Then he sat back, catching up her hands and pressing them with his as if he would never let them go.

He would never let *her* go—never again.

'I ask you to forgive me,' he said, his eyes searching hers, fusing with hers. 'For not understanding. For not knowing. For being so hopeless at realising what you meant.'

His hands pressed hers more tightly yet. Entreaty was in his eyes, his face.

'Forgive me, I beg you, but I didn't recognise love because I've never known it till this moment! Never in all my life experienced it.'

His eyes flickered for a moment, old shadows deep within them.

'They say,' he said slowly, 'that we have to be taught to love. And that it is in being loved that we learn to love.'

His gaze broke from her, looking past the trees around them, looking a long way past.

'I never learnt that essential lesson,' he said.

His eyes came back to her and she saw in them a pain that made her heart twist for him.

She pressed his fingers. 'Vasilis told me a little of your parents,' she said carefully, feeling her way. 'It made me understand you better, Anatole. And you yourself sometimes dropped signs about how unloving your parents were. Still are.' She gave a sad smile. 'Vasilis let me see how I'd wanted more from you than you could give me. He helped me to accept that you could not feel for me what I felt for you.'

'Felt?' The word dropped from his lips, fear audible.

She crushed his hands more tightly yet. Emotion

was streaming through her, pouring like a storm, a
tidal wave, overwhelming her with its power. But she
must find her way through it—find the words to tell
him.

'Oh, Anatole, I *made* myself fall out of love with
you! I had to! I had no choice. You didn't love me. You
could not love me! And I had to save myself. Save—'

She broke off. Then, with a breath, she spoke again,
her eyes clinging to his as she told him what had been
in her heart for so long.

'I fell in love with you, Anatole, when I was new
to you—when I was Tia. I knew it was unwise—but
how could I have stopped myself when you were so
wonderful to me, like a prince out of a fairytale?'

She looked away for a moment, her eyes shadowing, her voice changing as she looked back at him
knowing she must say this too. However difficult.

'Anatole, I give you my word that I never deliberately sought to get pregnant. But...' She took a sharp
breath, made herself say it. 'But when I thought I was,
I knew that I hoped so much that it was true! That I
was going to have your baby. Because...' She took
another breath. 'Because then surely you would realise you were in love with me too and would want to
marry me, make a family with me.'

She felt her hands clenching suddenly, spasming.

'But when you spoke to me—told me to my face
that if that was what I was hoping it would never happen, *could* never happen, that the only marriage you
could ever make would be an unwilling one, then...
Oh, then something died within me.'

A groan of remorse broke from him. 'That grue-
some lecture I gave you!'

Anatole's voice was harsh, but only with himself. He held her gaze, his eyes troubled, spoke again.

'Tia—Christine—I make no excuses for myself, but...' He paused, then continued, finding words with difficulty. 'I can only tell you how much I dreaded being made to be a father when the only one I knew— my own—was so totally and absolutely unfit to be one! Fatherhood was something I never wanted because I feared it so much. I feared that I would be as lousy a father as mine had been. But I've changed, Tia! I've changed totally!'

His voice softened.

'Meeting Nicky—feeling that rush whenever I see him, that incredible kick I get when I'm with him—oh, that's shown me just how much I've changed! Shown me how much I want a family of my own.'

She nodded slowly, her face working. 'I know— I *do* know that. Truly I do. But, Anatole, do you understand now why I had to refuse you when that was all you were offering me? I wanted to accept—dear God, how I longed to accept you!—but I did not dare.'

Her hands slipped from his now and she shifted her position, turning her shoulders away, her body language speaking to him of what speared him to the quick.

'I loved you once, Anatole, and lost you. I married Vasilis—not out of love, but... Well, it suited us.'

Did he hear evasion in her voice? She hurried on.

'All I knew was that to marry you simply to make a family for Nicky would have become hell on earth for me. Hell to know that I had fallen in love with you all over again and that all I was to you was a mother for Nicky, and a partner in your bed...' Her voice twisted. 'To be so close to heaven and yet outside the door still...'

He turned her to him, his hands warm on her shoulders. His voice was firm and strong, filled with a strength that came from the heart.

'I will make heaven for you, Tia. My adored Tia. My Christine—my beautiful, beloved Christine. My love for you will make heaven for you—for us both.'

Tears broke from her in a heart-rending sob and she was swept against him again. She clutched him and kissed him, his cheeks, his mouth, long and sweet and filled with all that she'd had to hold back from him. All that she need never hold back again.

He held her tight, returned her embraces, then sat back a little.

'Heaven for us *all*,' he said. 'You and me and Nicky.' His breath choked him suddenly. 'Nicky whom I will love as if he were my own.'

She stilled as if every cell in her body were turning to stone. Keeping her as silent as she had been for five long years. Then, beneath his gaze, she spoke. Said what she had to say.

Slowly, infinitely slowly, she picked each word with care. 'I have to tell you why I married Vasilis.'

She saw his features twist. Heard him make his own admission. So long denied.

'It hurt,' he said. 'I did not realise it, thought myself only angry with you. But that was because you'd left me for him—rejected me when I still wanted you. On my own terms, yes, but I wanted never to let you go.' He swallowed 'You wanted to leave me. And what he could offer you, I now understand, was more than I could offer.'

He took a ragged breath, met her troubled gaze.

'You wanted a child and so did Vasilis. It was that simple.'

She shook her head. A violent, urgent shaking. 'No—no, it was *not* that simple! Oh, God, Anatole, it was not that simple at all!'

Her voice was vehement, stormy with emotion.

'Anatole… That nightmare morning, when I told you I was not pregnant and you lectured me on how I must never let that happen, well…' Her throat closed, but she forced the words through. 'I was so terrified that I… I used the pregnancy test I'd been too scared to use before! I knew I didn't need to—that I had got my period—but I was so distraught that I wanted every proof I could grasp at! So I did the test—'

She stopped. Silenced by the truth she must tell him now. Her heart was like lead within her.

'It showed positive.'

There was silence. Silence all around. Even the birds were silent. Then…

'I don't understand.'

'Neither did I.' Her voice came as if from far away. 'Apparently it's not that unusual, though I had no idea at the time. There can still be a show of blood. Even when you're pregnant.'

His eyes were on her—staring, just staring. She went on—had to—had no choice but to do so.

'I was beside myself with terror. I knew I would have to tell you when you returned. How horrified you would be. And that was how your uncle found me,' she said, and swallowed, 'when he arrived for lunch with us.' Her face worked. 'He was so kind…so incredibly, wonderfully kind! He sat me down, calmed me down, got the whole dreadful tale out of me. How I'd fallen in love with you, but you hadn't with me, how you'd have felt you *had* to marry me, and how that would have condemned me to a lifetime's misery—condemned *you* too, ruining your life! How I loved you and knew I'd be forcing you to have a child you did not want, forcing you to marry me when you did not want to. And then…' she half closed her eyes '…then he made his suggestion.'

Another deep breath racked through her.

'He said that in the circumstances I needed time—time to think, to accept what had happened. Time to come to terms. To make my decision. Whether to tell you or to raise the child myself. So, as you know, he took me back to London, where I had more doctor's appointments to confirm that, yes, I was, indeed pregnant. And then…' She looked at Anatole. 'And then, knowing what I'd told him, and knowing you as he did, he offered me one other possibility.'

From far away she heard Anatole speak.

'To marry him so he could raise my son—the son I did not want. Marry the woman I did not want to marry.'

The accusation in his voice—against himself—was unbearable for her to hear. The pain was like a spear in her heart.

Her eyes flew to him. 'He did it for *you*, Anatole! To give your son a home, a loving and stable family, to provide for him and for me as his mother, in a way that was the very best way to do it!'

Her expression changed, infused with sadness now.

'He knew he would not live to see Nicky grow up, that he could only be a temporary figure in his life. That's why, as I told you, to Nicky he was his *pappou*. And for that very reason...' she swallowed again, making herself look at Anatole, hard though it was '...he knew that one day he would not be here. That one day—' she took a painful, harsh breath '—I would have to tell you. When the time was right.'

She was silent for a moment.

'And now that time has come, hasn't it, Anatole? Please, *please* tell me it has?' Her voice dropped to a whisper. 'Can you forgive me, Anatole, for what I did?'

His eyes were bleak. 'I am to blame,' he said. 'I brought it on myself.'

'You could not help the way you felt—the way you *didn't* feel!' Her negation of his lacerating self-accusation was instant.

He caught her hands. 'You are generous, Tia, but the fault is mine. That you did not even dare to tell me—' He broke off, anguish in his face.

She crushed his fingers in hers. 'Anatole, please! I understand. And maybe I *should* have told you. Maybe I should have had the courage, the resolution to do so. I've deprived you of your son—'

He cut across her. 'I didn't deserve him.'

His eyes clung to hers and she saw them change from self-accusation to something new.

Hope.

She said the words he needed to hear. 'But you deserve him *now*, Anatole,' she said quietly, from her heart. 'You have come to love him, and that is all a child needs. All that *you* were never given. And now,' she said, and her voice was choked with the emotion running through it, 'now Nicky is *yours*. Your son to love as he should be loved. As he *is* loved!'

She got to her feet, drawing him with her though she was so petite against his height. She gazed up at him, never letting go of his hands.

'And you will have a wife to love you too,' she said.

She lifted her mouth to his and his eyes softened, with a tenderness in them that lit her like a lamp.

'And you will have a husband to love you back,' he said gently.

His lips were a brush upon hers. His hands holding hers fast.

'Nicky is my son.' It was a statement—a truth that seemed to him to be opening the sky in a glory of brightest sunlight, blazing down on him. 'Nicky is *my* son!'

He gave a sudden great exclamation of joy, sliding his arms around her waist, lifting her up and twirling her round and round, laughing, exclaiming until he put her down again, breathless with joy.

'Dear God,' he said, 'can such happiness exist? To have discovered my love for you, for Nicky—and now to discover that you love me back, that the boy I've come to love is mine!'

His expression changed. Grew grave.

'But he is my uncle's child too. I will never forget that, Christine. I owe him that. And I will always be thankful to him for what he did for Nicky and for you.'

She felt her eyes fill with tears. 'He was a good man, my dear Vasilis. A *good* man.' And now her gaze was full upon him, 'Though he was never my husband in anything but name—he would not have wanted anything else, nor I.'

He was looking down at her, taking in the implications of what she'd said.

She gave a sad little smile. 'Did you never wonder why your uncle remained a bachelor? He was in love once, you know, when he was a student. But the woman he wanted to marry did not come from your world, and his parents objected. He resolved to get his teaching qualifications and marry her, be independent of the Kyrgiakis wealth. But...' Her voice became sadder. 'But, unbeknownst to him, while he was studying in England she found she was pregnant and developed eclampsia. They both died—she and the baby with her.'

She took a pained breath.

'I think, you know, that is partly why he offered to make me his wife—because he remembered how alone the woman he loved had been.'

Anatole folded her to him. 'Let us hope and pray,' he said quietly, 'that they are all finally together now. He and the woman he loved, and his own child.' He held her back, his eyes pouring into hers. 'As *we* are together, Tia—my beloved, my dearest adored Christine—as we are together now. You and me and our most precious son—together for ever. Nothing can part us now.' His voice seared with emotion. *'Nothing!'*

He kissed her again, sweetly and passionately, warmly and lovingly, and the world around them turned to gold.

It was Christine who drew back first. 'This is all very wonderful...' she said.

And there was a smile in her voice even as tears were in her eyes—tears of the radiant, unbreakable happiness and joy that swelled her heart until it was bursting within her at the miracle that had happened, at the gift she had been given that she had never hoped to have: the love of the man she loved...

'All very wonderful,' she repeated, her eyes starting to dance, 'but I really think we have to get back to the house. We have a trip to the beach to undertake! Or our son, Anatole—' did her voice choke over the word 'our'? She thought it did, and rejoiced in it '—our son will never forgive us!'

He gave a laugh as warm as the fire of happiness blazing within him and laced an arm around her. They walked back to the house—shoulder to shoulder now, and in all the days to come—ready to start their family life together.

EPILOGUE

THE LITTLE CHURCH was filled with flowers. But the guests were few and very select.

The Barcourts—with Giles's mother and sister looking particularly satisfied with events—occupied the front pew, and on the other side the vicar's wife sat with Mr and Mrs Hughes and Nanny Ruth.

As Christine progressed slowly up the nave, her pale lavender gown emphasising her slender beauty, she was followed by Nicky, holding her short train. He was followed by Isabel Barcourt's daughter as flower girl.

At the altar rail stood Anatole, waiting for his bride. As she reached him Christine smiled, turning to beckon Nicky to stand beside her. The vicar, his expression benign, began the service.

In Anatole's head Christine's words echoed. *'You would know it...'*

And now he did. He knew the power of love—the power that had brought him here, to this moment, where the woman he loved and the child he loved would be his for all eternity—as he was theirs.

Gravely he spoke the words that would unite them, heard Christine's clear voice echoing, until his ring was on her finger and hers on his.

'You may kiss the bride.' The vicar smiled.

She lifted her face to Anatole—to her husband, the man she loved. She let their mouths touch, exchanging their love. And then, with a graceful dip of her knees, she lifted Nicky. Anatole took him from her, hefting him effortlessly into the crook of his arm, and they both turned round.

The organ music surged, the bells pealed out, and the congregation burst into applause as the flower girl threw rose petals over them. Laughing and smiling, the three of them—husband and wife, mother and father and precious son—headed down the aisle and out into the golden sunshine of their lives beyond.

* * * * *

If you enjoyed
THE GREEK'S SECRET SON
by Julia James
why not explore these other books in the
SECRET HEIRS OF BILLIONAIRES *miniseries?*

KIDNAPPED FOR THE TYCOON'S BABY
by Louise Fuller
CARRYING THE SPANIARD'S CHILD
by Jennie Lucas
THE SECRET KEPT FROM THE GREEK
by Susan Stephens

Available now!

#3609 CASTIGLIONE'S PREGNANT PRINCESS
Vows for Billionaires
by Lynne Graham

Prince Vitale is driven by royal duty—until his hunger for Jazmine leaves her pregnant. A temporary marriage will legitimize their twins, but is the fire between them enough to make Jazz his permanent princess?

#3610 CONSEQUENCE OF HIS REVENGE
One Night With Consequences
by Dani Collins

When Dante fires Cami as punishment for her father's theft, he doesn't anticipate the temptation of her innocence! But what started as revenge could suddenly bind them forever when their inconvenient passion has long-lasting consequences...

#3611 IMPRISONED BY THE GREEK'S RING
Conveniently Wed!
by Caitlin Crews

After years of wrongful imprisonment, ruthless Atlas takes revenge on Lexi for putting him there. He'll bind her to him with a ring—for life! But her blissful surrender threatens to unravel his vengeance...

#3612 BLACKMAILED INTO THE MARRIAGE BED
by Melanie Milburne

Vinn wants estranged wife Ailsa back on his arm, and he's not above blackmail. But Ailsa meets his fire with fire, and Vinn must entice her with a scorching seduction!

#3613 VIERI'S CONVENIENT VOWS
by Andie Brock
Her runaway sister's agreement leaves Harper no choice but to marry Vieri! When passionately consummating their vows has consequences, Harper must decide: dare she trust Vieri with more than her body?

#3614 HER WEDDING NIGHT SURRENDER
by Clare Connelly
Pietro vowed to never seduce his convenient virgin bride—until the chemistry between him and Emmeline becomes undeniable. But while Pietro hides a devastating secret, can they be married in more than name...?

#3615 CAPTIVE AT HER ENEMY'S COMMAND
by Heidi Rice
Stranded in Italy, Katie is horrified when sexy billionaire Jared rescues her. He rejected innocent Katie once, but will the temptation of their burning attraction be too much to resist?

#3616 CONQUERING HIS VIRGIN QUEEN
by Pippa Roscoe
Odir is rightfully king, but he needs his wife by his side! Refusing to compromise power for passion drove Eloise away. Now pleasure will be his most powerful weapon in winning her back!

Get 2 Free Books,
Plus 2 Free Gifts —
just for trying the Reader Service!

His vengeance won't be complete until she's his bride!

After ten years in prison for a crime he didn't commit, ruthless Greek Atlas Chariton is back to take revenge on Lexi Haring—the woman who put him there. He'll meet her at the altar and bind her to him—for life! But once they're married, the bliss of her sensual surrender threatens to unravel his hard-won vengeance…

Read on for a sneak preview of
Caitlin Crews's next story
IMPRISONED BY THE GREEK'S RING
part of the **CONVENIENTLY WED!** miniseries.

Atlas was a primitive man, when all was said and done. And whatever else happened in this dirty game, Lexi was his.

Entirely his, to do with as he wished.

He kissed her and he kissed her. He indulged himself. He toyed with her. He tasted her. He was unapologetic and thorough at once.

And with every taste, every indulgence, Atlas felt.

He felt.

He, who hadn't felt a damned thing in years. He, who had walled himself off to survive. He had become stone. Fury in human form.

But Lexi tasted like hope.

"This doesn't feel like revenge," she whispered in his ear, and she sounded drugged.

HPEXP0318

"I'm delighted you think so," he replied.

And then he set his mouth to hers again, because it was easier. Or better. Or simply because he had to or die wanting her.

Lexi thrashed beneath him, and he wasn't sure why until he tilted back his head to get a better look at her face. And the answer slammed through him like some kind of cannonball, shot straight into him.

Need. She was wild with need.

And he couldn't seem to get enough of it. Of her.

The part of him that trusted no one, and her least of all, didn't trust this reaction, either.

But the rest of him—especially the hardest part of him—didn't care.

Because she tasted like magic and he had given up on magic a long, long time ago.

Because her hands tangled in his hair and tugged his face to hers, and he didn't have it in him to question that.

All Atlas knew was that he wanted more. Needed more.

As if, after surviving things that no man should be forced to bear, it would be little Lexi Haring who took him out. It would be this one shockingly pretty woman who would be the end of him. And not because she'd plotted against him, as he believed some if not all of her family had done, but because of this. Her surrender.

The endless, wondrous glory of her surrender.

Don't miss
IMPRISONED BY THE GREEK'S RING
available April 2018 wherever
Harlequin Presents® books and ebooks are sold.

www.Harlequin.com